Lonely People Meet

Lonely People Meet

Sayantan Ghosh

BLOOMSBURY
NEW DELHI • LONDON • OXFORD • NEW YORK • SYDNEY

BLOOMSBURY INDIA
Bloomsbury Publishing India Pvt. Ltd
Second Floor, LSC Building No. 4, DDA Complex, Pocket C – 6 & 7,
Vasant Kunj, New Delhi, 110070

BLOOMSBURY, BLOOMSBURY INDIA and the Diana logo
are trademarks of Bloomsbury Publishing Plc

First published in India 2025

ISBN: PB: 978-93-69524-13-6; eBook: 978-93-69523-63-4
2 4 6 8 10 9 7 5 3 1

Typeset in Bembo by Manipal Technologies Limited
Printed and bound in India by Thomson Press India Ltd

MIX
Paper | Supporting responsible forestry
FSC® C010615

To find out more about our authors and books visit www.bloomsbury.com and sign up for our newsletters

For sale in the Indian subcontinent only

To learning how to say no, na, nein, nee, nyet

Prologue

WHEN ANANDA REZA CHOWDHURY migrated to Delhi from Dhaka many moons ago, all he wanted was to write for a living. Three decades later, now in his mid-fifties, he still lived to write, but it was never enough to pay his bills. So, like many writers before and after him, he also taught at a college. He lived on the fourth floor of an apartment complex in Vasant Kunj with his partner of a few years, Suneeta, who was an active member of one of New Delhi's oldest theatre groups. Ananda had a moderately social life, but he despised social media and was openly critical of anybody with an X account. He hated giving interviews or even being in the public eye.

The day his car got stopped at Nelson Mandela Marg for overspeeding, he wasn't the one in the driver's seat. Suneeta was. It was a long stretch of road with very little traffic. They had stepped out for lunch and were on their way back home. Suneeta liked taking a quick nap before her evening rehearsals, so she was going a little over her usual speed. Ananda usually didn't drive, because he felt that all cars in Delhi existed for the sole purpose of bumping into his. 'This isn't a city meant for driving; this is a city made of striking cars and unlucky pedestrians,' he would say.

A couple of cops appeared in the distance and signalled them to stop the car. Suneeta looked at Ananda sheepishly and saw him roll his eyes and look away. Ananda always preferred taking a cab and had suggested they take one that day too. But Suneeta wanted to drive and had insisted they take the car out for a spin.

As she stopped under a tree, next to which were parked two motorcycles, she watched one of the cops throw away the cigarette he was smoking and approach their car. She rolled down the window on her side and apologized to the policeman before he had even said a word.

'*License hai*?' the man questioned.

Suneeta nodded.

Then he looked at Ananda's disinterested face and asked, 'I think I have seen him somewhere. Your husband? Is he famous?'

Suneeta remained silent, but Ananda looked at the man and said irritably, 'If I was, then you would have let us leave by now, Officer. Whatever it was, it was surely a minor mistake. We didn't jump any signal, and there's no car in sight other than ours.'

Anybody who has ever dealt with the police in this part of the country knows that that is not how you *ever* talk to cops in North India.

The man laughed like men who take themselves too seriously often do when they feel affronted. '*Challan toh kätega*,' he said.

'But why, Officer?' Suneeta already knew the answer but asked nevertheless.

'Overspeeding, madam,' the cop said nonchalantly. 'The speed limit on this road is fifty, and the rule is the same for everybody. So you don't go treating it as your own property and start racing here whenever you please.' That irked Suneeta, but she tried to remain calm.

'Do whatever you need to, and please let us go,' Ananda responded quickly, but he sounded too defiant for someone who had just agreed to pay a fine.

The man straightened his well-worn shirt and asked them to wait. Then he walked towards the other officer who was standing near the parked motorcycles. This second guy had been staring curiously at Ananda all this while, which the couple had not noticed. When the first cop reached the spot and asked him to take out the challan book, both Ananda and Suneeta observed him pointing towards their car and saying something.

In a few minutes, they were both near Suneeta's window. This time, however, Suneeta and Ananda were asked to step out of the vehicle. The two men in uniform seemed both alarmed and exasperated but tried not to let it show.

'You're that writer, aren't you?' one of the cops asked.

Ananda replied in his usual sardonic tone, 'There are thousands of writers in the world. What do you mean by *that* writer?'

The other officer, noticeably younger than his partner, asked Ananda for his phone. When he refused, they explained that their cell phones had had no connectivity since morning, and they simply wanted to verify something on the internet. Suneeta whispered in his ear, 'Just give it to them and let's get this over with.' Ananda took out his phone from his pocket and handed it to the younger cop. The two stared at the screen together as he typed something, and presumably finding the page they were looking for, they went over it with a look of concern. Then they turned the phone towards him.

An article Ananda had written in a national daily a week ago had gone viral, which he had been blissfully unaware of until Suneeta had informed him. He had nodded after hearing her and gone back to watching a cricket match on the TV.

The piece, which was widely shared, discussed and debated in various circles, was on police brutality – a reality that, unfortunately, resonates with most disenfranchised communities in India. Not to forget protesting students as well as common citizens who have had to often take to the streets to raise their voice against the state's failure or subjugation – who are no longer surprised to find riot police at peaceful marches and gatherings, or by water cannons and lathi-charges.

This is the world we live in now. But this is also how the world has been for as long as one can remember. From the Vietnam War protester who placed a carnation into the barrel of a rifle, to the unidentified man who stood in front of a column of tanks leaving Tiananmen Square, to Saffiyah Khan who smiled fiercely at an English Defence League protester in Birmingham – these fault lines are ancient. No great societal transformation in human history has transpired without large-scale civil disobedience.

When the older officer showed Ananda his phone, the article was open on it. The image accompanying it was of an unarmed man confronting a pistol-wielding policeman in Hong Kong, taken during the violent conflicts which had occurred in October 2019.

'*This* writer,' he said.

Ananda took a quick glance at it and then looked the policemen in the eye. 'Should I be flattered or scared that you've read my column?'

'You hate us hard-working folks because of whom you feel safe in this city, don't you?' they asked.

'Don't be silly!' said Ananda. Suneeta grabbed his arm and pressed it firmly to indicate that he shouldn't be using such language. He continued in a more restrained tone, 'I don't hate anybody. This is a critique, not a hate piece. If you read it carefully, you will understand that I am not demonizing everyone wearing a police uniform but pointing out various flaws in the system, which cause some guys to behave irresponsibly and, if I may say so, even dangerously.'

The younger cop came forward and said, 'Don't you try to mislead us. Many of my friends forwarded it to me. I felt so embarrassed.'

'Which part of the essay bothered you?' Ananda asked impatiently.

'What do you mean?'

'Which line, which passage, which thought in the essay upset you so much? Show me that part, and I'll tell you why I have written it. Maybe that will help us understand each other better,' he said.

This was a new challenge thrown at the young man, the kind he wasn't used to. Their usual culprits were those who would either threaten to call a politician or try to bribe their way out of the soup they had got themselves into.

'How will I know?' the young man replied, mildly confused. 'I haven't read it.'

'You have a problem with a piece you haven't read?' Ananda laughed. 'You're a funny guy.'

It was evident to Suneeta that Ananda's brazen dismissal of the authority of these two protectors of law wasn't sitting well with them. But Ananda wasn't wrong. They were trying to bully him into submission. And he refused to take that lying down. People who can't handle hecklers shouldn't write viral pieces in a post-2014 India.

She imagined their own faces in the next day's newspaper; first as front-page news with a headline in big, bold letters but soon settled with a small piece somewhere inside – maybe a one-hundred-fifty-word column on a page no one read, added as an afterthought.

It was now the senior cop's turn to take over.

'What do you mean by that?' he came forward and asked in a chillingly calm voice.

'By what?' Ananda said.

'What do you mean that he's funny? Is he a clown? Is he a jester appointed by the government to entertain you?'

Ananda was startled and replied cautiously, 'Now you're just trying to put words in my mouth. I didn't say any of that.'

The policeman sighed. 'But that is what you're implying, aren't you? That we are mere jokers in front of you – in front of a learned, distinguished and privileged gentleman like yourself!'

Ananda was taken aback. Is this how institutional scapegoats are found and made? Out of thin air, on the quietly violent, empty streets of a giant metropolis? He felt bad for himself but remembered what this friend of his who lived in Srinagar always told him: 'Whenever you think that there's too much injustice around for you to bear, think about Kashmir and you'll feel better.'

'I am not looking for any trouble. Let us go, please,' he said.

The cop smirked when he heard this. 'Oh, now you're saying please. The nobleman is pleading to the court jester? What did we do to deserve this honour?' he said. Then he derisively looked at the phone screen again. 'This … this is the part which bothered my friend the most,' he said, pointing at the essay's byline that read 'Ananda Reza'.

It hadn't been long, but both Suneeta and Ananda felt tired of these uniformed men. As though they had been participating in this confrontation for years. Suneeta held Ananda's hand firmly; they couldn't deny the dread that had made a home in their hearts in the past few minutes. Has either of these young men heard the name George Floyd? The man who lost his life for twenty bucks and was killed by a knee? Or Breonna Taylor or Michael Brown, or closer to home our very own Jayaraj and his innocent son Fenix? Suneeta wondered.

'What do you want from us?' Ananda asked, his sweaty and tense palm in Suneeta's.

'Just tell us why you find my friend here funny, and you're free to leave.'

Suneeta tried to intervene and said, 'He didn't mean it that way, Officer. He was only—'

'Did I ask you, ma'am?' the man interrupted her, as he began rolling up his sleeves. She stared unwaveringly at the man's shirt; the several sweat patches on it seemed to have drawn the map of a nation where some people roamed in khakis and many spent their whole lives in prison cells.

The man turned towards Ananda once again and said, 'What do you think young children will learn from you if they see you laugh at the police of their great country, sir? All those impressionable minds, going to the best schools and colleges – where people like us can never go – tomorrow's leaders, doctors, intellectuals and celebrities. Is this what you want to teach them? So your cycle of leftist hate remains well oiled and continues to go forward?'

Ananda wasn't sure why the man decided to include the word 'leftist' in their conversation. He wanted to say something, but the cop cut him off. 'You know what I actually find funny?' he said as he raised the phone in his hand and brought it so close to Ananda's face that the letters on the screen blurred and became illegible. 'This,' the cop said. 'This liberal propaganda which you're trying to spread through such articles. I find *this* hilarious.'

Ananda knew arguing with him was pointless. 'What do you want me to do?' he managed to say.

'Say it with me,' the officer said.

'What should I say?'

He pointed at the phone. 'Say that every word you've written here is funny. Because if it isn't funny, then it is slander – an attack against the country – because these uniforms represent the state. You look like a decent man. Do you want us to believe you're an anti-national element, sir?'

Ananda and Suneeta had seen this violence many times, on their TVs and their cell phones – but never so closely before. They had once watched a documentary which had even shown them how things unfold in real time from the point of view of the one getting attacked. All of earth had become a found-footage film.

'I bet you also remember the order in which the Mughal kings ruled in India,' he continued.

Ananda's article didn't mention any of these things. And yet all these unrelated concerns were being coupled together – like a puppeteer from above wanted them to form a club. Patriotism, propaganda, liberal, leftist, slander, Mughals … Reza … Muslim … anti-national. Go burn together with them if you dare.

The irony was that Ananda did know the order like the back of his hand. He went to a Bengali-medium school until the tenth standard, and one Mr Bakshi, his history teacher, had taught his class this trick. He remembered the sentence.

Babar holo abar jawr, sharilo aushawdhe.

'Father was down with fever again, medicine cured him.' A seemingly pointless statement, but the magic lay somewhere else. The first letter of each word in the original sentence was the first letter of the name of a Mughal emperor. And that too arranged in the order of their rule.

Babar … *Babur.*

Holo … *Humayun.*

Abar … *Akbar.*

Jawr … *Jahangir.*

Sharilo … *Shah Jahan.*

Aushawdhe … *Aurangzeb.*

Ananda wished he could teach the officer this simple trick too. So he wouldn't forget history – and try to help rewrite it for his children. And those who will come after them.

But his heart knew better, and he kept quiet.

Involuntarily his hands went up, like he had seen fugitives do in countless films. Even though nobody had asked him to.

Then they all heard a whimpering sound and found it was Suneeta who was finally falling apart.

'Not so funny now, is it?' the policeman said.

Then the man dropped Ananda's phone and pretended it had slipped by mistake. It fell face down on the gravel. The phone's screen smashed into pieces in an instant. His article was now invisible.

When they finally made it home, they were one phone less, but their bodies were intact. In complete silence they moved around the house for the rest of the day – managing chores, picking up a chair and placing it somewhere else, filling up the bottles with Aquaguard water at the kitchen counter – hiding from each other while sharing the same roof.

That night when Ananda lay down on their bed, he remembered the missed calls from his daughter that he hadn't returned earlier. Suneeta had never married, and Ananda had Neela, his only daughter, from his previous marriage. He borrowed Suneeta's phone and dialled her number. An excited voice picked up the call saying, 'Baba, I'm coming home to see you next month.'

Ananda knew he was supposed to feel thrilled but replied instantly, 'No! Don't.' Perhaps she couldn't completely comprehend his response for she didn't say anything.

Those few moments of silence gave Ananda the opportunity to think about the enormity of the dread he was experiencing, and how human beings were no longer secure anywhere. But he couldn't find the strength to speak. After she hung up, he sent her a short text, which read: *I'm sorry, maa. See you soon!*

As he closed his eyes, thoughts of a girl he had once known pervaded his head, someone who would have stood up to those bullies – who would have taken the bullet if she had to but wouldn't have behaved like a puppet in front of them. She, who always raged against the dying of the light.

When sleep finally came, he dreamt he was lying in a pool of his own blood. His heart was beating, his eyes were open, and his fingers twitched. But he wasn't alive.

1

KARNO PLUGGED THE EARPHONES into the jack of his mid-range mobile phone in a flash and took off. It took an extra two seconds, but it was important for him. He had heard the woman scream after the thief had snatched her purse and fled moments ago. One glimpse of her face, clearly visible under the raging Delhi sun (also thanks to her hair that was firmly tied back), and he knew that she was possibly his type. Or at least the idea of a type he had been carrying around in his head for decades. Not someone he just fooled around with or took home to meet his parents or had intellectually stimulating conversations with in the middle of the night after watching Jordan Peele's latest film. But all of this in one person. Someone who could complete his unfulfilling life.

Now he was no fool. The naivety of this expectation wasn't lost on him. But he also knew that life would become an unbearable exercise without the necessary distractions. And this, this pursuit of a perfect person who would fit into his life like missing links in a chain – there was no better distraction than this.

Imagine playing a video game. As long as you keep losing, there's always a reason to press the 'Try Again' button. Once you win, some voice or a neon sign on the screen sends you a congratulatory message and praises your valour and glory. But for how long? Two seconds? Maybe five? Ten? Or twenty? Maybe for a minute? Then what? You may switch the game with a new one, but there's no guarantee that it's going to engage you as much as this one. You were engaged, certainly. Why else would you want to see the end of it? But as long as you keep failing, there's no such fear. As long as your battleship keeps crashing seconds before victory, you have a reason to wake up and get ready to fight again.

This search for the perfect person was Karno's battleship – fighting a losing battle which kept him going.

Now he was off.

Karno was a failed marathon runner who occasionally ran a bookstore. He didn't own it. Not like Hugh Grant in *Notting Hill*, the charming bookstore-owner next door. Not Karno. He only managed it once in a while.

He was running against the wind as the clustered lanes of Daryaganj and the djinns who live in the Jama Masjid nearby whooshed past him. He could see the man in a black hoodie bumping into the rickshaw pullers as he ran like a mad horse. It was winter in Delhi. Everyone was in a black hoodie. If he didn't keep his eyes steady on the thief, he'd surely lose him in no time.

Besides, this could be a whole network of pickpockets. He could have a friend waiting for him at the next corner. So, if Karno were to catch him, it had to be before he took that next turn. Before he handed over the purse to someone else – the purse that belonged to the one he thought could be the woman of his dreams – and disappeared in the hustle of an overpopulated megalopolis. This wasn't just a race, but as the Hollywood wallahs liked to call it, it was a race against time.

Should he turn and look at her face a second time to determine if this struggle was really worth the trouble? No, like he was no Hugh Grant, he was no Milkha Singh either.

He thought of all the editions of *What I Talk About When I Talk About Running*; their covers mostly showing a lone man in shorts running. He had seen five, perhaps six different versions of it on the internet. He owned two of them. Maybe this girl whose purse he was after owned a third kind. If they joined lives, their home libraries would also be combined. And then he could have one more edition of his favourite book. If she was a reader, of course. But Karno had learnt to trust his heart in the thirty years he had spent keeping it in a cage. He knew it wouldn't lead him to someone who didn't love books.

That was all the push his feet needed. They picked up steam, and he foresaw his hands on the thief's neck in the next fifteen seconds. And he managed to get to him in twelve.

In no time, that man was lying on the road. His hoodie was covered in dust and smut. He would need a good detergent to get it all off. But it wouldn't be bought from the cash inside the wallet he was holding in his hands. Not that Karno didn't think of landing a punch on his face for his misdemeanour, but the boy – he couldn't have been more than sixteen or seventeen years of age – dropped the purse in front of him and folded his hands asking for mercy.

Karno picked up the purse and then gave the boy a hand. Before an angry mob could gather around them and ask the boy his last name or religion to decide his fate, Karno gave him a quick hug and asked him to walk away slowly. Like your parents advised you when as a kid, you told them about the mad dog in your neighbourhood. If you run, it will chase you. If you wait for the right moment and walk away slowly, the dog might let you go. India's mob is an angry mad dog today.

It wasn't a purse. It was a tote bag that had 'Shakespeare and Company' written on it. The bookstore of his dreams in Paris. That hit the nail hard on its head. Not only was she a lover of books but she had also been to the very bookstore James Baldwin once used to haunt to clear his writer's block.

She had touched the stones of its walls and breathed the same air Ezra Pound and Ernest Hemingway had once breathed. Because he was certain the air inside that store must have stood still for years. Like time certainly had.

Unless it was a friend's bag which she had borrowed today. But why that day? Of all days? Unlikely, he thought.

One day this had to happen. One day his stars had to align. Why couldn't today be that day? Just because he had idlis for breakfast?

As he walked back towards her, he thought about the number of possibilities that lay ahead:

a) She thanks him, takes the bag and leaves before he can say a word.
b) He hands her the bag, she checks it quickly to see if anything is missing, the trust is broken, they turn and walk away from each other and never meet again.
c) She takes the bag, exchanges numbers, agrees to meet later.
d) She takes the bag, exchanges numbers, agrees to meet later, gets crushed under the wheels of a moving bus five minutes later and that's that.

There she was, in a green dress, waiting for him. Waiting for her bag, really. But he came with it, like a backup dancer in a bad Bollywood song. She couldn't have one without the other.

But she took him by surprise.

She took the bag from Karno and said, 'My heart is broken. I'll keep the bag, but you can have the book inside it if you want.' He liked the fact that she assumed he liked to read.

'Which book is it?' he asked.

She brought out of the bag a paperback edition of Jonathan Franzen's *Freedom* and hung the bag on her left shoulder.

'You hate this book so much?'

She said, 'I don't hate or love this book. But I want to forget the one who gave it to me. That's why I didn't even go after that thief and just stood here, unsure if you were chasing him or were a part of his gang.'

'Then why did you scream?'

'The scream you heard was an involuntary reaction, come on. But right after that I thought that it won't be such a bad way to get rid of it.'

Karno nodded and said he didn't mind keeping the book.

'I got my heart broken too,' he said. 'Last year.'

'Someone left you?'

'Yeah, that is the ideal way to describe what happened. She just got up and left one day. No fights, no warnings, no telltale signs of a relationship that has ruptured beyond repair.'

'Why?' she asked.

'She changed a lot from when we first met. And I did not change at all.'

She laughed. She had the laugh of a self-assured person; someone who possibly didn't need to lock herself up in the bathroom to stop her hands from shivering before stepping out of the house.

'Is it too much information too soon?'

'I guess,' Karno said.

'I hope you didn't hit the guy who was running away with my bag.'

'No, in fact I gave him a hug. Thanks to him I am meeting a woman for the first time in months and not on my phone screen but in real life.'

She laughed again. 'Let's get together sometime then.'

She didn't say meet. Like most people do. He noticed that. She said 'get together'. Like forming a team, not merely participating in a casual encounter. He was already being proven right inside his head. She is the one he has been waiting for. But it's too early to tell her that. Especially not in the middle of the road. He thought he would tell her soon though, perhaps when they 'get together' later.

But where?

'There's something peculiar I like to do on Wednesday,' she said. 'You should come along.'

And he did.

'4 p.m., outside Green Park metro station. The one that is near the Indian Oil building.'

'I'll be there,' he said. 'But hey, tell me your name.'

'Devaki.'

They met outside the station as planned. Standing on the pavement next to a bustling street, she asked him if he thought that the Indian Oil building had drums of oil stored in its basement for an oil emergency that might occur in the future. He thought for a second and replied that it was most probably against some security protocol to store so much oil under a building where hundreds of workers were working; if anything went wrong, the fireworks to follow would be enough to engulf all of Green Park.

She felt he was exaggerating.

'What are we doing here?'

There's this thing she said she does sometimes. She would pick a random spot in the city and stand there. Until her eyes met someone who she thought could have an interesting life story. Someone passing by, getting a bus, sharing a cab, or buying medicines or flowers. Just regular people. But those whose stories she would feel might be worth knowing. And then she would follow them.

'Follow? What … follow where? Like on Twitter?' he asked naively.

'I don't use social media,' she said.

And before they knew it, they were walking fifty metres behind another couple, maintaining a safe distance but staying close enough to hear them talk; two people they had never seen before in their lives.

City life takes a lot from its dwellers but often offers anonymity in return.

Briefly, they discussed if following somebody was acceptable behaviour or not.

'It's the same as the internet, Karno,' she said. 'You follow, you dig, you stalk.'

'But it's not the same thing,' he argued. 'On the internet, everything is public. On the internet, you're aware that you're laying your life out for the rest of the world to see and judge.'

The question of consent arose. Hackers excluded, of course.

She didn't buy it though. Being disagreeable was one of her principal qualities, she said. 'Everything that's happening outside your head is public, K. There are no secrets in the world,' she stated matter-of-factly.

The couple was arguing. It's part of the deal. When you join hands with someone, whether in business or love, you must learn to find a silver lining in arguments. Since the two things are inseparable, and because it's inevitable.

They entered a small park where middle-aged men jogged in the evening to reduce belly fat, then gathered outside its gate at the kulfi stall to eat kulfis and bitch about how their wives didn't satisfy them any more.

The oblivious couple sat down on a bench under the shade of a neem tree. Devaki and Karno sat on a bench which had its back towards the couple's bench.

They sat far enough from them to give them the illusion of privacy and yet were close enough to hear what they were saying to each other. She was pregnant with his kid. He wanted her to keep it; she had other plans.

He pleaded with her every few seconds to change her mind.

She resented him for doing so. But with the nonchalance of someone who would have been disappointed if he hadn't.

'Isn't this an odd idea for a first date? Certainly, it's the oddest one I have ever been on,' said Karno.

'Are we calling this a date already?' said Devaki.

'Aren't we?'

'Well, I barely know you. Forget about going on a date, you're too much of a stranger to even have a meal with.' She chuckled.

When they tried to listen again, the couple was talking about life and death, and the man said they have no right to decide who lives and who dies, and the woman said the creator gets to take that call.

The man was listening to her mutely. Then he gently moved the hair that had covered her face after a sudden gust of wind came from the south … and then he told her that it made him very sad to think that she felt that way.

'You don't have to be sentimental about it now.'

'Is that what you think this is?' he said, the hurt in his voice apparent.

'We are ill-equipped for parenthood, don't you see?' she said. 'We went too far without thinking and that's got us here. And now we must stop and retrace our steps.'

'It's too late for that now,' the man countered. 'We will be destroying something that didn't ask to exist in the first place.'

'What doesn't have a consciousness doesn't have rights, baby,' she tried reasoning with him.

'How do you know it doesn't have a consciousness?'

'It is common knowledge; it is barely days old.'

Both sounded like students in a classroom – studying, learning something new about life together.

We educate ourselves to the best of our abilities. We read books, we teach books. We make notes, we share notes, we even compare notes. And just when we start thinking that all our actions are based on information we have already verified and memorized, we come to realize that so much in life is based on hearsay.

'Common knowledge can be incorrect too. It's not necessary that what we have believed for decades or even hundreds of years is true. That's why the world keeps changing.'

'There's no consciousness without pain or suffering, try to understand,' she said. 'And without a consciousness the question of rights does not arise. It's like dismantling a machine. It doesn't feel, it doesn't know.'

Then he stared into her liquid eyes and said, 'We are not gods, honey.'

Then there was silence. Devaki got up and decided to leave at this point.

'Don't you want to know what decision they come to?' Karno asked.

'It's not for us to know,' she said. 'Like their child, it's also their secret to keep from us and from the world.'

'Okay, can we go somewhere else now? Please?' Karno said.

'We are,' said Devaki.

Devaki left the scene as easily as she had entered, and they decided to see each other again a few days later. And it was there, in that rickety coffee shop in Connaught Place, called Madras Coffee House, where Karno said to her that they should get to know each other better. It was

Karno who had picked their meeting place this time. She had never been there before and curiously fixed her gaze towards one of the damp walls with its plaster tearing off; a characteristic feature of most decrepit Delhi buildings. The high ceilings made every sound echo.

'Have you ever seen someone drown, Karno?' she suddenly asked.

It was the strangest thing anyone had ever asked him. A close second would be that time Murli, his dearest friend in school, had asked him in the eighth standard if he had ever eaten the ice cream part of a Cornetto and then jerked off inside the cone. Karno's best friend was Murli, and the irony wasn't lost on either of them.

'Have you, Karno?' she asked again.

Karno shook his head. 'Why? Have you?'

'Yes. During our summer vacations, we used to visit my grandmother in the village in Bengal where her ancestral house was. Among the local kids who I had befriended, there was a lively young boy; I think everyone used to call him Jamun, because he loved eating blackberries so much. Everyone said he was an ace swimmer. So the day he climbed a tree next to a pond to pick mangoes and fell in the water, no one bothered to look. Even when he didn't come up after a few seconds, all of us who were playing near the pond thought he was joking with us. By the time some of the older boys felt it had been too long and jumped in, it was already too late.'

'That's just terrible,' Karno said.

'That's not the saddest part, K,' she said, her gaze intact. He treasured that minuscule fraction of a second in which her mind must have decided to replace Karno with K and wanted to tell her how strangely joyful that made him feel.

'Four days later, the villagers found his body. It was not even a mile away from his own home. But he had simply vanished for those four days. As if he had fallen through a deep cleft inside the earth.'

She continued after a pause.

'What do you do when you're lost so close to home? And are not found when you need to be found?' she said.

Karno couldn't decide what could be an appropriate response to what Devaki had just narrated, so he closed his eyes and invited her home. 'Will you … come home … some day?'

She was, in every sense, a strange character. She accepted Karno's offer but insisted he also call a few of his friends and introduce them to her. Karno wanted to spend time alone with her, but she seemed persistent. Could it be that she thought he would expect them to have sex if they were alone in the house? But the thought hadn't crossed Karno's mind even once. It was not that he wasn't attracted to her. He was, and amply so. But he had rushed into forming attachments too many times in the past and suffered, and this time he wanted things to be different. He wanted things between him and Devaki to grow at their own pace, even if it seemed languid at first. They had met in the aftermath of a chase, and now they deserved slowness. He didn't feel the instant desire of puppy love which convinces people to seek immediate companionship. Instead, he wished this to be like catching a slow-moving train. One that's about to leave the station, the whistle has been blown, but there's enough time to jog alongside before finally grabbing the handle and taking the leap.

Obviously, Devaki was unaware of all of this. Karno's thoughts were only a part of his own world. They had just met a couple of times, and he was already asking her to come home. In her mind, he was still somewhere between a friend and a potential rapist. He decided to call over his only two friends in the city. She seemed delighted, more than he had expected her to be. It almost felt like she had agreed to come over only to meet them.

When she met Rhea and Sandip, she transformed. There was the same electricity in her eyes, but her smile was consistently wide throughout the evening. That she made a conscious attempt to charm them wasn't too hard for Karno to notice. No wonder she won over the room so easily. It wasn't that she became a different person. But the manner in which her body swayed around the house, as she moved from one conversation to another – from the price of potatoes in the market to Leonard Cohen's last love letter to his beloved – if someone had told Karno that she had been possessed by the ghost of an optimistic stage performer, he wouldn't have doubted them. Karno wasn't complaining, but something told him that this performance would not continue once the guests left; that her usual quiet would return, which he had already begun to miss. But with it would also leave this eagerness to venture outside one's skin and be a part of a joyous moment. *Why do we never feel contented with what we have*?

They opened the wine bottle which Rhea had brought along, and that's when Karno first learnt that Devaki did not drink.

'You don't?' Karno asked.

'Not anymore,' she said.

Most of his adult life was spent warming up to members of the opposite sex after downing a few, which made it easier for him to communicate. But in the case of Devaki, he realized, he would have to lay his guard down without any outside support. Of course, he could still get a few gin and tonics down his throat before being intimate with her, but it's not the same thing if the other person is not riding the same boat.

Sandip, who was part of a jazz band, had brought his guitar along with him, which he started strumming after dinner. When he asked Devaki what kind of music she liked, she said she was not into music but one of her exes was. She had never mentioned an ex, not that Karno had asked. But Devaki slipped her name with so much ease into that conversation that it almost seemed like Faiza was sitting right there with the rest of them.

'Faiza used to play the guitar too on some days, and she had a playlist for every occasion.' There was no place for envy in their equation yet, so Karno distracted himself by thinking about his cricketing days when he was still a teenager. Whenever he needed a distraction, he always chose to take his mind off to a cricket pitch and placed himself in a hypothetical situation, like a character in a video game. Three overs left and seventy-nine runs to make; six deliveries to bowl and defend just one run; three balls to face and each must be hit for a six – all most unlikely to happen in the real world. But in his head, he always managed to navigate these mazes and come out victorious. When he couldn't sleep, which was on most nights, he did the same thing.

Later that evening, she lay on top of him. They were both fully clothed, but Karno had never felt this kind of intimacy before in his life. Their eyes didn't meet, their bodies were stationary – like a freshwater lake after it has rained. She mumbled something which he couldn't follow, so he asked her to repeat herself.

'Am I the first chance encounter of your life which is this memorable?' she asked.

It was an unusual question. Perhaps she was. At least no other memory came to his mind. 'Yes, I guess you are.'

Her head on his chest moved a little, as if to trace an indiscernible shape on his shirt and then went back to being as still as it was before. He wished in his heart that the shape was a smile.

'Am I yours too?' he asked expectantly. A question that could mean a million different things. 'You can tell me if I'm not.'

She thought for an extra second and said, 'You are, you know. But a few months ago I was at the metro station and there was a man on the platform who was looking inside a file and mumbling to himself. I went closer to him and stood there and only then realized that he was an actor of some sort who was rehearsing his lines. It was just so warm, that whole scene unfolding in front of me. He had a hat on, and a brown shirt and a ragged pair of denims with mud on them. He almost looked fictional.'

Karno smiled.

'Our eyes met, and I said hello. He did the same. We talked for a few minutes until the train arrived. He said he was auditioning for a part in Girish Karnad's *Tughlaq*. He was on his way to the audition and incredibly nervous. I asked him if I could hold his hands for a minute; they were shaking, like they do when someone has been out in the cold for too long. And he let me. And we stood like that for a few minutes, his trembling hands in mine. My hands trying to comfort his like I was warming the body of a tiny rabbit. Soon the train was there; he said, "Wish me luck," and got on it, before turning around to say a final goodbye, but the doors had already closed by then. I could only see one of his hands waving at me, the one I had cured just moments ago. And the train left the station while I stood there watching it go. I should have been on it too. But I took the next one because I didn't know how far I could travel with that stranger. Sometimes I wish I had taken that train with him.'

Next evening she took him to Lodi Gardens. Despite living in Delhi for almost five years, Karno hadn't ever been inside the place. They held hands like old lovers do, not with youthful vigour but naturally, as if out of habit. His hand sliding into hers as he breathed in a chest full of what seemed like clean air – something that was becoming scarcer than osmium every year.

She asked him what his story was.

They had not done this bit yet. Usually that's what people do when they meet for the first time. Over a drink or dinner or during a walk after watching a film. But they had met under unusual circumstances.

Karno came from, what one would call, an upper middle class Bengali family. His grandparents on both sides had crossed the Bangladesh border during Partition and settled in Bengal. Both his parents were born in Calcutta, and Karno too was born and raised there.

His was one of the most ancient stories.

Karno's self-made businessman father had trouble understanding why his only son was not interested in inheriting his business and wealth and instead wanted to become a writer. He was always a quiet child, never made many friends, but his father took that as a good sign. He thought his son would have less distractions, and it would be easier when the time to pass the mantle finally arrived.

His parents were in an unhappy marriage but not the kind in which they couldn't stand each other. They let each other be, didn't feign affection and never fought in public.

Karno's uncle, his father's younger brother, owned a small apartment in Hauz Khas so Karno didn't have to pay rent every month. During his first two years in Delhi, he took up some freelance editing jobs through friends and acquaintances and managed to make a living. Since then, he had been working on the first draft of a novel but hadn't had the conviction to share it with anyone yet. And apart from the periodic editing assignments, he managed to write the occasional essay for a few national dailies. And then there was the bookstore where he often spent a large part of his day, watching young students browse through books – only to take photographs of their covers to order on Amazon later – and walk out. It's not how Karno had imagined things would turn out, but he had managed to build a somewhat decent life for himself in this unforgiving city, and there had been no reason for his parents to call him back home. At least for that he was grateful.

Then it was Devaki's turn to speak. Karno had always been a good listener. They sat down next to a tree on the lush green garden bed from where they could see the Bara Gumbad – constructed in 1490 CE during the reign of the Lodi dynasty, believed to have the earliest constructed full dome of any building in Delhi. This city belonged as much to the dead as to the living.

Devaki said her story was a little more complicated than his. That's how she started it. It always annoyed Karno when someone used the word 'complicated' without irony. Especially when about someone's life or relationships. *It's complicated.* What did it even mean?

Was she born in Auschwitz that her life is complicated?

Did she watch Mt Fuji erupt and destroy a civilization while she was eating breakfast one day?

Does she know the exact day the world would finally end? Because anything less didn't cut it for Karno. Or so he thought.

Strangely, she skipped through several years of her life and began talking about the time when she was in college. Which Karno guessed couldn't have been more than half a decade ago.

'I was deeply in love with someone who I thought understood me,' was how she started. And here he was, still trying to write an unforgettable first sentence for his novel even after years of struggle.

'She … taught literature in the college I went to, but I was not in her class. She was, in fact, one of the youngest assistant lecturers who taught in our college, but I read psychology. I saw her in the corridor every morning, and on some days she noticed me too. We would nod at each other, pass a smile sometimes; once our hands brushed against each other's, but she was on a phone call and didn't realize. But I did. I noted and hoarded the memory of every single instance when our paths even accidentally crossed. Some days I followed her home. She lived in an apartment building, which was about a six-minute walk from our campus.

'Then one day it was raining heavily and the whole city was flooded; we were receiving messages from friends not to step out because all the streets were waterlogged and there weren't enough vehicles plying on the road. It was July, I remember. I hadn't seen her all day that day. I was too bored to stay in college; classes had been cancelled anyway. I was standing outside the campus gate and trying relentlessly to find a cab for myself, when I saw her walk past me, and as soon as our eyes met, she said, "Hey".

'I froze for a moment, but she continued and asked me what I was doing out in this bad weather. And I said to her, "But you're out in the rain too." And she laughed and said, "Oh, that's only because I live just around the corner." I pretended that I didn't already know that. Just then a gush of wind snapped one of the metal rods which were keeping my umbrella intact, and there I was at the mercy of Mother Nature and a literature scholar I had lost my heart to. She must have noticed the cab company app open on my phone because she said, "Why don't you come over and wait at my place until your taxi arrives …?" And I instantly knew either something wonderful or something dangerous was about to begin. Little did I know some things could be both at the same time.'

Devaki spoke as if she had forgotten to breathe in between. Such was the miraculous flow of her words, crashing on the shore like waves on a full moon night. If only he could write as effortlessly, Karno thought. But he couldn't tell whether this was a story she repeated so many times that she knew its every word, every turn of phrase, each element by heart, or if she was narrating it for the first time and couldn't wait to let it out to someone.

'Pizza?'

Karno was startled, as if a dream was interrupted. 'What?' he asked. 'You went to get pizza in that rain?'

'No, silly,' she said. 'Order pizza now, to eat here. I have been talking and talking, and the body needs something cheesy.'

For the first time since they had met, she seemed like any other person, who liked talking about old loves and eating cheese. He took out his phone to place the order, while she began humming a Phil Collins tune which he had last heard in his teens, when his mother used to play audio cassettes on the Philips two-in-one stereo they owned. It's as if the story, her own story, had opened some valve in her heart and pumped fresh blood into it. He asked her what kind of pizza she liked, and she answered, 'Pepperoni,' without hesitation. Once he was done, he put his phone back inside his pocket and said, 'Hmm … let's continue.'

She looked at his face, his eyes and nose and beard, his chin and ears, and the folds on his forehead, as if she was touching each part with her eyes, and she smiled with a kind of gentleness common only to truly fulfilled people.

'We reached her two-bedroom apartment that was on the third floor. She always liked living high up, she mentioned. Every floor took her farther away from the streets below; she told me how much she hated car horns. She brought me a towel to dry my hair and went inside. Two minutes later, she stepped out with two glasses and a bottle of gin in her hand. The tonic was inside the refrigerator next to the couch, where I was sitting, she told me. I instantly got up to fetch it. It was about five in the evening, and I would usually have a cup of coffee at this hour. But there was a calming assurance in the way she walked out with the two glasses and that bottle of Gordon's which made me not want to challenge her expectation and ruin the moment. I forgot about the fact that I was supposed to wait at her place until my cab arrived; instead, I silenced my phone and put it inside my backpack. Maybe the driver arrived, waited, called and then cursed me before eventually leaving. I don't even remember. How do people know when is the right time to leave? Some people, I have heard, have premonitions – people who get off a bus which later falls into a river or those who know which lottery ticket to buy so they win. I wish I was such a person, then I would have picked up the driver's call and left in the cab that day.'

2

KARNO SUFFERED FROM A specific kind of despair which had prevented him from getting too close to people in the past. When Karno was fourteen, his parents mutually decided that they should separate. But they didn't know how to break the news to young Karno. He would have had a breakdown, felt shattered and even betrayed at the thought. So they did what most Bengalis do when they are in a fix and can't reach a decision. They booked a room in a hotel in the Darjeeling hills in North Bengal and drove down to spend the weekend there. Darjeeling also used to be Karno's favourite spot, and the plan was to let him savour the experience of spending a couple of days there with both his parents by his side and disclose the truth to him only on the morning of the day of their return.

Karno sat in the back seat throughout their journey. Usually, he was used to taking his Walkman and a bunch of English rock cassettes with him whenever they drove out of town. His mother liked listening to Jagjit Singh's ghazals, and his father liked old Bengali film songs. There was enough conflict as it was, and he didn't wish to impose Jim Morrison or David Bowie on top of it. Instead, he would plug in his earphones and cut himself off from the world. Only his eyes would capture the sun shifting positions outside their Maruti's window and the miles and miles of yellow farmlands passing by. Once in a while, he could see a man walking beside a water buffalo tilling his land; huts would appear occasionally. The music blasting in Karno's ears, he would turn the volume up each time he would see his parents' mouths move, fists clench and their brows turn into sea waves, anticipating war, forgetting that he was right there, an arm's length away from them, visible in the rear-view mirror.

Ground Control to Major Tom
Ground Control to Major Tom
Take your protein pills and put your helmet on

He wanted to call out to Major Tom, but he knew Tom couldn't hear him. It pained him to think that his capsule was floating in outer space, farther and farther away, far above the moon somewhere. Until Karno realized that he was the one sitting in a tin can, his was the voice which no one could hear. Then he was numb for some time.

The weekend passed quietly. Karno refused to go sightseeing and spent most of his time at the Oxford Bookstore on Mall Road. He bought Che Guevara's memoir *The Motorcycle Diaries* on the day they arrived and finished reading it in the next two days. Naturally, there wasn't much talking that happened between parents and child. He was mostly found sitting on a green bench next to a railing overlooking the hills on Mall Road, and on one of the afternoons he fell asleep on it, turning the paperback into a pillow. Until he was woken up by the sudden chill that often surrounds mountain towns when the sun begins to go down.

In a way, he had become used to hearing his parents bicker continuously. Sometimes he felt they looked for reasons to be unpleasant around each other. It was as if they were suffering from a shared illness – a case of folie à deux, a condition they had simultaneously developed perhaps by watching one another. Not every ailment necessarily has a biological cause. Hundreds of refugee children in Sweden had reportedly fallen into coma-like states in the past few years when they were informed that their families would be deported.

The only thing Karno's parents didn't blame each other for was the weather. They felt the same way about the rain. They both hated it. Plans were cancelled when it rained, and they had to stay indoors, inside the same house where the other was. Theirs was a small house then – this was before his father's business had taken off. One bedroom, one living room, one kitchen, one bathroom and the refuge of a balcony overlooking a lane which flooded during the monsoon months.

They both hated monsoon equally. Except on the day when Karno was born. It rained heavily all over Calcutta that day too. But he was told how exhilarated and optimistic they both had looked – his twenty-two-year-old promising mother, Mala, and twenty-seven-year-old ambitious father, Asim. From the stories he had gathered, told by his grandparents, friends of his parents and neighbours, he had managed to piece together a picture in his mind. A picture of them sitting on that hospital bed, his mother in an overused hospital gown, and his father in a worn-out maroon T-shirt, which Karno had seen him wearing in some other photographs too, holding Karno in their arms, together. Their four hands indistinguishable, dissolving into one whole, as if no one who saw them that day would have been able to guess where one's arm ended and the other's began. And at the centre was Karno, the final vertex of the triangle, who was meant to complete them. If only it hadn't rained so much that day.

When Karno woke up on the morning they were going to leave Darjeeling, he found the room they were staying in empty. There was a note on the bedside table in his father's handwriting which said, 'Get ready quickly, see us at the lawn, have ordered coffee and sandwiches for you.' It was no mystery to Karno that the conversation which was to follow would be an uncomfortable one. When parents say they know their children better than anybody else, they often forget that their children know them equally well. And in some cases, like Karno's, even better.

Karno took a bath as instructed, wore his favourite white shirt with little brown foxes showing various moods printed on it, and stepped out of the room. His heart was ready to bear a storm. All he wished was for his face not to betray him – he hated it when others knew how he was feeling just by looking at him.

His father, who never minced words, began with the punchline, 'Your mother and I are getting a divorce.'

Karno took a sip of his coffee which had already gone cold and looked around quizzically to see if any of the waiters was bringing his sandwiches to him. Mountains make some people hungrier. Perhaps at high altitudes, where oxygen levels are low, one tries to fill the empty spaces in the lungs with morsels of food. No such cure for the heart though.

'Don't you have anything to say?' he asked Karno.

'I do,' said Karno. 'Since the sandwiches are not here yet, can I have a croissant instead?'

His parents looked at each other in shock and awe. *What is wrong with this kid?* The question was written all over their pale faces – exhausted from not having yelled at each other in the last forty-eight hours.

'Did you even hear what your father just told you?' said his mother.

'I did,' Karno said calmly.

'AND YOU WANT A CROISSANT?' said his mother, not able to keep her voice down any longer.

Karno sighed and said, 'Will my having a sandwich make you change your mind? Because then I will. Then I will have a sandwich all the remaining days of my life, Ma, every morning, without fail.'

His parents kept looking at him in disbelief, now overpowered by a sudden sense of shame at having raised a boy like Karno who seemed to care so little. He went on, 'But you have made up your minds about not staying with each other. You had made up your minds long ago or maybe when we were driving down to this place in the car, when you were seated next to each other, one with his eyes on the road and one looking out, pretending you couldn't see the other.' Then he waited for a second and said, 'I had made up my mind about the croissant when I was coming down the stairs.'

Karno heard them finish their tea in silence after that. Neither the sandwiches nor the croissant came. Then his parents got up and left for the hotel room together. He sat on the wrought iron chair on the lawn of the hotel his father had picked for them without consulting either him or his mother, and he stared at the cliffs at a distance which made him think of his own life … shadowy, hazy, indiscernible.

Karno waited for about fifteen minutes, which seemed to him like many hours, and then walked up the wooden stairs of the hotel, past giant portraits of the owner's grandparents followed by parents who ran the property before him. Karno knew the owner was a man because his own portrait, the largest of them all, was hung behind the reception area in the lobby. His name shone in a garish gold-plated font – Ranjit Kumar Chaudhary. What is it that makes someone display their family tree in this fashion? Pride? Or a sense of belonging? Or a record of personal history which serves as a dispatch for all guests and visitors that success isn't found in a day; that only by carrying the baton your ancestors have passed on to you can you truly belong to the idea of a family. What was he to take from his parents that he would want to pass on to those who would come after him? Did Ranjit Kumar Chaudhary ever hear his parents fight?

When he stood outside the door of their room, Karno could hear his mother sobbing. But there was no urgency in that whimper. It came in spurts, as if minutes passed between one tear and the next. He placed his hand on the steely doorknob and turned it cautiously. As he pushed the door open, he could see his parents sitting on the queen bed, which was still unmade, beside each other. Karno hadn't seen them be physically so close to each other in months, maybe even years. His mother's head on his father's shoulder, a cascade from her eyes making a blot on his shirt as if quenching its thirst. His father's arm gently wrapped around her like a December blanket.

Karno's feet felt sweaty. It seemed to him like a scene from an old film he hadn't watched. A middle-aged man in a suede jacket and a woman in a cotton saree busy in an embrace. His mother spoke first. 'He's our fault. Neither of us can abandon him now or he'll sink.'

They were talking about him even though they had a mountain of other worries to deal with, which they had been keeping aside for a long time. But at least they were talking. 'We won't,' his father said. 'He has failed us because we failed him first.'

Duh, Karno thought.

Karno stood at the door and listened to them for some time. They didn't notice him. Or even if they did, they didn't acknowledge his presence. If he had an audience, he could have convinced them that he was an apparition. Asim and Mala discussed their son's future, his grades at school which were continually deteriorating, him even losing interest in his piano lessons which Mala had wanted him to learn because she couldn't when she was young. Perhaps they spent too much time smashing decorative items their home didn't need or yelling at each other because they had no common objective left to speak about. Maybe they needed the volume, the clamour, because their arguments were devoid of even the faculty to be suitably accusatory. Like a blank space between two words, like the lull after an explosion.

But suddenly that had changed. Their only son, in a brief moment of insensitivity, had exposed himself as a faulty project which they needed to fix. And they had to do it together. On their way back to Calcutta, Karno couldn't remember if he even said a word. But both his parents were their most talkative selves that day. They debated, bickered, calmed down on their own when a heavy gust from the river bed next to the winding road ambushed their white Maruti and enfolded them. Karno's father spoke about the need to spend more time with Karno. His mother reminded his father that Karno needed to be less afraid of his father's everyday rage. In those thirteen or fourteen hours in the car that day, Karno took the fall. But he couldn't recall the last time he had been so much at peace with himself.

Sometime around dusk, as the car raced through the heat and dust of rural Bengal, Karno laid his head gently on the backrest and remembered the time when a stray cat had entered his grandparents' house and made it her home. For a few weeks everyone was okay with an intruder among them, who sometimes behaved like she was the landlord of a house in which they were tenants.

Then one day, his grandmother noticed that the cat was pregnant, and she panicked. They were getting old, and they didn't have the energy or ability to handle more than one feral companion. They requested the man who worked as a driver for them to take the cat and leave it somewhere far from their house so she couldn't find her way back. They all knew it was an act of cruelty. But one that had to be done to ensure their own lives' balance wasn't disturbed.

Karno saw Gopal, the man entrusted with the job of seizing the cat and putting it inside a gunny bag and then driving off with it. He returned an hour later without the cat or the gunny bag. Gopal wasn't a violent man by any means. But that day Karno had a hunch that maybe Gopal had killed the cat, perhaps unintentionally asphyxiating it by tying the mouth of the gunny bag too firmly. Then three months passed, and everyone forgot about the cat. Until one day, the cat returned to their neighbourhood, with three kittens. A woman, who lived with her infant son next door, gave them shelter. Surely the mother cat recognized Karno's grandparents' house, he thought. She had spent a good few weeks there. She knew every corner, every corridor inside that house. She had even found herself hiding spots for when she wanted to avoid people totally. She had made it her home. One she owned and ruled over. But after she returned from her exile that day, and every day since, when she stayed next door, she never once turned towards his grandparents' home. In abandonment she had found the strength to renounce her memories.

That evening, in the car, Karno forgot the precautionary practices his parents had tried instilling in him all his life and stuck his head out of the window to let the wind dissolve every human voice he had ever heard in his whole life. And in that moment, he felt luckier than the cat.

3

WHEN YOU HAVE SEEN things fall apart around you at a very early age, staying faithful to the idea of togetherness becomes a task. Even before Devaki had finished telling her story that day, Karno had concluded that her heart lay silently by Faiza's side. Faiza never taught Devaki in any classroom, but she became 'Prof' for her. And Devaki let go of her appendage and became 'Devi'. Together they were teacher and goddess – ready to take over the world.

This was many years before that historic day when cities turned into rainbows in this country. Their love then was so forbidden that it couldn't be interrogated until it was claimed, because to even question that love meant it had to be spoken about, and such profanity was not acceptable yet to the general Indian on the street.

Nobody raised an eyebrow when they walked hand in hand in public, because what else could they be but sisters? Or best friends, or colleagues who have grown fond of one another only because they see each other every day. Their love was forbidden but only when announced. Otherwise, as 'sahelis', they could breach boundaries, laugh at staring men together and cheer for each other, lie on the other's lap under the stars in the green gardens of Purana Qila. But not kiss. Not when there were eyes watching. Their intimacies were limited to palms, elbows, shoulders, knees, toes – their eyes were allowed to wander wherever air touches our bodies, but lips were meant to stay apart at all costs. And they were happy to reserve it for moments of privacy.

Inside the campus they maintained distance. But after six, every evening, Devaki would be at Faiza's apartment. They managed to discover a unique symmetry in their communication which never allowed them to get bored of each other. There was no grand declaration of love, because what they felt was a concoction of care, lust, attraction and affection. It didn't call for a certificate. They didn't realize how quickly time passed when they were together, and that was enough.

Faiza lived in Uday Park, and on Saturday afternoons they would walk to Jughead's and pick up cheap Chinese food, then stay locked up in her bedroom for hours.

Devaki's father had passed away when she was barely two, and her mother lived in Kanpur with her uncles. Her duties involved calling her mother twice every day, once in the morning and once before going to sleep at night. In the hours that fell in between, she was all Faiza's.

Devaki hadn't moved in with her, but no matter how far she went from Faiza's house every day, she always had the heel of one foot inside her door.

'Am I a burden to you?' Devaki would often ask her.

Faiza never answered that question. She would continue doing what she was doing – cooking, reading, looking into her phone or looking out the window. On some days, she would smile and hold Devaki's hand fondly while humming a ghazal, and sometimes she would simply ignore it altogether, like the question was never raised at all.

Only once did Devaki refuse to take her indifference for an answer, so Faiza had to respond.

'You slow me down, Devi.'

'What are you trying to say?'

Faiza smiled and, taking Devaki's face in her hands, said, 'When you are around, I forget to run.

'There's an American photographer named Thomas Joshua Cooper. Have you heard of him?'

Devaki shook her head.

'He's old and frail now but risks his life for taking each of his photographs to this day. I read somewhere that the camera he uses is a five-by-seven-inch field camera, which is essentially a wooden box that was built way back in 1898. It is heavy and fragile and makes his life difficult, for he has to carry it around to the locations where he shoots. But he refuses to leave it behind and lugs it to every corner of the earth. His labour brings him happiness, because it is born out of love. Trying to protect it from the world has proven near fatal for him on a few occasions, but he refuses to adapt to the modern ways of doing things. At least when it comes to taking photographs. He calls it "baby". That's who you are for me. My aberration. My exception. My annihilation. My labour of love.'

It was a Friday evening in September. They had planned to go out for dinner at a Japanese restaurant that Faiza really liked. The intense summer heat of Delhi had started giving way to a mild nip in the air. Faiza rarely made plans which involved stepping out of her pyjamas or the house. So, when she texted Devaki – 'Get home by 7, let's go to Kofuku tonight' – Devaki was excited and pleasantly surprised.

'All okay, Prof? :D' she wrote back.

For a few minutes her phone didn't buzz. When she was about to put it back inside her jeans pocket, it beeped. 'Can't write. Need inspiration. Something to break the mind clutter. Hence, sushi.'

Devaki was in CR Park at a college friend's house. She looked at her watch and saw it was ten minutes past six.

'See you at 7,' she wrote back. Then she picked up her bag and rushed out after giving her friend a quick hug.

But the first thing you learn when you move to Delhi is that you must never trust the city's weather and its traffic. By the time she reached Uday Park, paid the auto driver, and walked up the stairs of Faiza's apartment, the hour hand of her wristwatch was already nudging eight.

She immediately put on her apologetic face and hugged Faiza as soon as she opened the door. Faiza preferred to maintain a mental timetable every day, and Devaki knew that if it got disturbed, Faiza turned into an extremely caustic and bitter person. At least for some time. It was the last thing she wanted after getting stuck inside an auto-rickshaw for almost two hours in the Delhi grime.

'I'm sorry, Prof. Really not my fault,' she said.

'Don't worry about it. Come, sit.'

Devaki couldn't believe her ears for a second.

'Really, you're okay with this? That we are an hour late for our plan tonight?'

'Yes.' Faiza kept the latest edition of the Bangla magazine *Desh* on the coffee table, which she was reading before the bell rang, looked at Devaki and smiled.

'I don't understand, am I not late?'

Faiza said, 'Actually, you're three hours early.'

'Early? How?'

'We'll only leave around eleven.'

Devaki displayed mild amazement on her face and said, 'And why is that?'

'Because our train leaves only at midnight. We're going to Benaras.'

When the thoughts of delicious sushi melting in her mouth had done nothing to help how listless and uninspired Faiza felt all day, she asked herself what's the one thing that would, if not enthuse, at least calm her thumping heart inside her chest. And she remembered the Ganga Aarti on the Dashashwamedh Ghat in Benaras which had left her entranced years ago, when she was around Devaki's age. She could hear the conches, she could sense the aroma of the hundreds of incense sticks alight together, she could see the numerous diyas floating in the distance, sailing away from her.

That day she saw a thousand diyas with her eyes closed and each had a word written on it. 'Return', 'Music', 'Fever', 'Mausam', 'Pīnas', 'Phagun', 'Megh' and nine hundred and ninety-three others. There were names of loved ones written on them; there were names of cities which one had left behind, names of villages one would never go back to. Everyone on that ghat had written their favourite word on a diya and set it free into the river. Faiza knew it was her mind playing tricks. But in that instance, she chose to believe this treachery. As if all these words would be swallowed by the sea that night, when everyone was asleep, and the day the sea engulfs every living being on this planet eradicating life from it, only a poem shall remain. A poem made of those thousand words that set sail at that moment in front of her eyes.

That's all it took.

Faiza knew a travel agent who owed her a favour from long ago. He had booked two tickets for a two-tier compartment of the Bhrigu Superfast Express for her at no extra cost and had emailed them to her before Devaki had arrived at her house with a sorry face. The train would reach the Varanasi Junction station by noon.

Inside the train, they were seated opposite a middle-aged couple, who not for once looked at the two of them with suspicion. *Sisters*, they assumed – giving immediate proof of it when the fifty-something man tried to initiate small talk with them. And, as is the case with most Indian men, it happened without subtlety and within the first twenty minutes after the train had left the Anand Vihar Terminal railway station.

'Travelling with your sibling, is there anything more fun than that in this world?' he said with a beaming smile on his face.

Neither of them flinched.

'It's a gift that keeps on giving,' Devaki said.

And then she pursed her lips to stop herself from grinning, which might have blown their cover if Faiza hadn't added, 'But you may have noticed, there's a considerable age difference between the two of us. So we are also like mother and daughter sometimes.'

'Of course, of course,' said the man.

This difference she spoke of was not more than nine years. But on Faiza's weathered face each of those years doubled themselves, often making it difficult for strangers to gauge her correct age.

'But for the most part, we are each other's confidante and travel companion, so we are also like friends.'

Devaki knew where Faiza was going with this.

'You must see us when we fight! Like *sisters*, you know?' Most people could have sensed the sarcasm in her voice from a mile away. But that poor man, unused to women taking control of a conversation, wasn't as lucky. 'We fight, then we stop talking, we even avoid looking at each other and that's when we become total strangers.'

The man was now looking towards his wife, hoping she would find an entry point into this exchange and somehow rescue him. But Faiza was in a certain type of mood that day – tired yet unforgiving, with a hint of mischief reflecting in her eyes, noticeable only to Devaki.

'And as you must have guessed by now, we love each other immensely. Perhaps more than you love your wife. So, we are lovers too.' Then she laughed.

The couple left them alone for the rest of the journey. Except in the morning, when it was time for breakfast, and they unpacked the food – parathas and pickle – they had carefully carried from home in steel tiffin boxes. The woman leaned forward with one of the boxes and offered some to Devaki and Faiza. Devaki refused saying she wasn't used to eating in the morning, but Faiza thanked her with a smile and took one paratha. She tore a piece and dipped it into the pickle before putting it in her mouth and exclaiming how wonderful its taste was. The woman's husband maintained a stoic silence. There's this thing about Indians – no matter how hostile the atmosphere in the room is, once the lids of tiffin carriers come off and food is laid out on the table, it has to be shared with everyone present. One of those rare traditions which deserves more credit than it gets.

After they got off at the Varanasi Junction station, the woman waved goodbye to them but didn't wait for a response before turning and walking away holding her husband's arm. Faiza had already booked a room for the two of them at a Hotel Surya. They walked out of the station, hailed a local taxi and left for their destination.

At the reception, a young man greeted and welcomed them courteously. His senior stood behind him, overseeing, while he checked the details of Faiza's booking, asked for their identity cards and photocopied them with precision for hotel records. As the receptionist handed Faiza the key to their room, the older gentleman decided to make a quick point.

'Welcome to Surya, ma'am. We will ensure you have a great stay with us and are able to go back and tell your friends and family about Surya's hospitality.'

His words had the dullness of someone who has been confined to a prison cell for an eternity and has scribbled the same sentence on its walls over and over again, and a sincere but laboured politeness which only comes to people who are used to wearing uncomfortable suits.

'In case there is something you need, please feel free to call the reception desk or room service. You will find all the details in your room, on the bedside table.'

Faiza thanked him, while Devaki said to no one in particular, 'I already quite like the ambience. It is quieter than the rest of the city. Otherwise, everything outside is so chaotic here.'

'We take pride in the ambience we provide to our clients, ma'am,' the man said. 'We strictly ensure there is no nuisance inside our premises, which is why our policy is to only give our rooms on rent to families. This is neither a cheap hostel for college kids, nor a lovers' den.' He impressed himself so much with that last statement that he laughed rather loudly, startling the young receptionist.

There it was again, that old, accustomed feeling of dealing with the world's blindness towards their love, exposed and served like a buffet for a country of fools unacquainted with aspects of their own culture and history.

Faiza, who was already walking towards the elevator, stopped, turned around and politely asked, 'So you think we are related?'

Now there was some confusion on the man's face, and as if his younger assistant was instructed to shadow the man's every move, the same confusion reflected on his face too.

They exchanged quick glances and then the man said, 'You are not?'

'I asked you,' said Faiza, looking straight at him with a hint of a smile.

'Well, I assumed you two are cousin sisters. But now that you've planted a seed of doubt in my mind, I would say you could be family friends too.'

'And what makes you say that?'

'I don't know, madam. You could say it's a calculated guess. Or it's just experience – years of standing behind this counter and welcoming new guests every day.' He tapped his fingers on the counter.

'You have intuitive powers then, I must say, Mr …'

'Oh, I completely forgot to introduce myself,' he said. 'My apologies. Myself Manohar Lal Hooda. I am the manager of this hotel.'

'… Mr Hooda,' Faiza finished her sentence.

Then Devaki saw something shift on Faiza's face and realized she was probably going to correct him but not before subjecting him to her acerbic wit. She swiftly moved in front of Faiza and intervened, saying, 'You should have been an astrologer, Mr Hooda. You really can read faces.'

Hooda, not surprisingly, was very pleased to hear this. 'Actually, one of my uncles is an astro …'

Devaki cut him off before he could go on about his uncle any further and said, 'If we need any assistance now, we'll know who to go to. Thank you, once again.'

Hooda figured they were not interested in his family history and said, 'Anytime, ma'am. Please don't hesitate to call. Hooda is here for you. You please go ahead; I'll send someone with your luggage to your room.'

Devaki thanked him and his stupefied junior once again and got inside the elevator, pulling Faiza's hand to ensure she was with her. Once the door of the elevator closed, they looked at each other and broke out into childlike laughter.

They hadn't been together for very long, merely a few months. But there are all kinds of couples in this world. Some who end up spending a major part of their lives together and yet know very little about each other, living like acquaintances who have been sentenced to stay under the same roof. Then there are those like Devaki and Faiza were, who had learnt to read each other's silences and laughter in no time.

4

THE MORE KARNO HEARD about Faiza and Devaki, the more removed he felt from Devaki; the more unwanted, uninvited and immaterial his presence seemed in her life. Yet all he sought was her company and approval. He wanted to become important in her life; like a Virginia Creeper climbs up the walls of an old manor without support and envelops it completely in the blink of an eye, he wished their lives to become as indistinguishable from each other.

'Didn't you once say that you work in a bookstore?' she asked out of the blue. 'Do you ever go there?' Then with just the precise amount of saltiness, she added, 'Since the time I have met you, I have never heard about you going to any bookstore to work.'

'I used to, quite regularly …' said Karno, '… until I met you.'

'When have I ever stopped you from going there? Or working?' Devaki snapped at him.

Karno smirked and said, 'Of course, you haven't. In any case, I don't do that bookstore gig for money. I do it to spend more time around books and because Intezaar Sahab, who owns the place, likes me a lot. I go there whenever I can, to keep him company, learn about new and old titles, and at the same time sell a few, if possible. He gives me twenty rupees for every book I manage to sell to a customer. So you see, the money I make isn't a lot. But the joy of seeing someone discover what could perhaps become their favourite book is unparalleled. I wouldn't trade that for anything. Except that now I like spending the excess time I get with you. That's where I would go to earlier, whenever I was done with my freelance work deadlines. Now I come to you. Or you come to me.'

She hardly took an extra second to think and then said, 'Okay, let's change that then. Take me to the bookstore tomorrow. You can work, and I will help. And if I can't help, then I will browse books and watch you work.'

Next morning at the store, Intezaar Sahab hugged him and then took a moment to look at his face like we sometimes look at the photograph of a loved one whom we will never see again.

'Where had you disappeared, you fool?' he asked, but there was less resentment in it and more … what does one call it in English … For some words there are no literal translations that can do justice to their meanings. *Abhiman* in Hindi. *Obhiman* in Bangla. That is the word. Google will say it is the same as 'pride'. But it isn't. It is a more nuanced feeling than that, and you can only partake in it if there's ownership involved.

Devaki noticed that Intezaar Sahab's store didn't really require an extra worker, like how Karno didn't need this 'job'. There were enough people to dust, maintain stock, and, if needed, to climb a ladder to take out a book from the top shelves in his dainty little shop. While Intezaar Sahab himself manned the cash counter. Its odd rectangular shape was overflowing with books, with a wooden staircase thrown right in the middle of the room, which was taking up some serious space. And once you climbed it, another Pandora's Box opened – full of more books, more dust and a low ceiling that made every movement inside that matchbox-shaped room a challenge. A challenge one would only regret not accepting.

But that didn't mean they didn't need one another. This dependence, or whatever name you give to it, was more visceral, more organic in nature. Like a cat needs a box. The only rationale for such behaviour is the prospect of a public space suddenly turning into a safe zone for those involved – when the cat jumps inside the cardboard box or when Intezaar Sahab pulls Karno, who's almost half his age, into a tight embrace.

Karno introduced Devaki to Intezaar Sahab as his close friend, and he, very gently, placed his right palm on top of her head and said a little prayer.

Devaki smiled and said, 'This is my first time here.'

Intezaar Sahab held her arm like a family elder would and said, 'From now on, you are always and forever welcome here.'

She saw him 'hand-sell' a Rilke at eleven, the English translation of an Omani novel at noon, and a bunch of Amitav Ghosh titles at a quarter past two to an enthusiastic geriatric who, to everyone's surprise, said he had never heard of Ghosh; proof that even if you become the most famous person in the world, there will always be at least one person somewhere for whom you will be a total stranger. Surely there's some comfort to be derived from that thought.

'Hand-sell' is apparently a popular word with booksellers across North India, Devaki learnt later. As if there's another part of one's body that one can use too to sell a book to a reader.

If it was up to her, she would 'armpit sell' the books, Devaki whispered in Karno's ears, so that Intezaar Sahab wouldn't hear her.

Karno laughed and said, 'It really means when you manage to get a reader to buy a book they weren't interested in and hadn't intended to purchase at first.'

'You explain so well, K,' Devaki replied.

Karno, who was busy rearranging the horror shelf, didn't realize that she was mocking him, and said, 'Thanks!'

Devaki laughed and said, 'So why don't you sometimes try to put that skill to better use other than stating the obvious?'

Then Karno turned around to look at her and meekly said, 'Sorry, sometimes I can be really daft.'

Around four in the afternoon, when Karno was sitting upstairs on the timber floor, among the Kunderas, Sontags, Calvinos and Lispectors, dreaming of meeting Annie Ernaux someday, Intezaar Sahab prudently asked Devaki, 'Why don't you ask him to finish his novel, beta? He certainly is a gifted writer. I know because I have read some of his work. He never shows me anything, but I make sure to search his name on the internet once every few weeks, knowing that a new article by him will most likely pop up.'

Karno had mentioned to Devaki once that he was working on a manuscript but wasn't prepared to share it with the world yet. Devaki had decided to not probe any further and wait until he felt ready.

That day she felt a strange pang of sympathy, a sudden bout of affection for Karno. She walked up the small stairs unhurriedly and sat next to him, surprising him by putting her head on his shoulder.

'Have you been writing?' she said.

'Why? Did Intezaar Sahab say something?'

'How does it matter, K?'

He turned towards her and said, 'How does it also matter if I am writing or not?'

Devaki moved her face away from his collarbone, which was touching her lower lip, and sat up straight to look at Karno. 'Have you forgotten why you moved to Delhi, K? You moved to this city to become a writer, didn't you? Isn't that what you say to everyone who asks you this question? Isn't it important that you fulfil the promise you made to yourself that day when you sat on the train, leaving your home, your mother and, most importantly, your city behind? Don't you owe it to yourself? And to all the things you gave up just so you could do this?'

Karno appeared lost and forlorn. Devaki had never seen him look like this before. It reminded her of that scene from *Annie Hall* where Alvy Singer, one of the protagonists, says, 'I feel that life is divided into the horrible and the miserable. That's the two categories.'

'What's the point, Devaki?' Karno brought her out of that trance. 'There's already so much art in this world. So many writers have already produced thousands of wonderful books – many of which are never read, many of which you and I will never read. Some we don't even know the names of, even if they have managed to change some people's lives somewhere on this planet. What's the use of adding to that number when we haven't even been able to consume what exists already?'

'You sound like a defeatist, K.'

Karno continued, unaffected. 'Plus, there's the internet, D – such a vast, never-ending universe. Information is free there. If someone has to pay to read, especially for pleasure, it needs to be extraordinary, doesn't it? That shouldn't be the exception to the rule, but an obligation.'

An hour later they were out on Aurobindo Marg, walking towards a sandwich shop in the Hauz Khas market where they served Blue Tokai coffee, which both Karno and Devaki often craved.

Devaki picked up where they had left off.

'But you and I both know that the internet is controlled by a few conglomerates. Sure, when it was invented, it was meant to connect the world and make it a better place, but today it's a tool for some five big companies in the world to manipulate our needs and convert them into wants so that they can sell their products or services. Any information that's free cannot be a hundred per cent genuine, K.'

'There is no doubt in my mind that the internet manipulates us, D,' Karno said. 'Just as there is no doubt in my mind that before the internet there were television commercials and before that there were radio advertisements; we're still bombarded with print ads every time we open the morning newspaper, just like it used to be long before the radio was invented. What I'm trying to say is that our quotidian needs have always been influenced by advertisers, in one form or another.'

Devaki sighed.

'But billboards and flyers cannot refashion personal taste.'

As they took their seats at the sandwich shop, Devaki ordered an espresso while Karno asked for a cup of filter coffee. The air inside the cafe tasted musky. Over the course of the next hour, Devaki spoke about a disconcerting 'fact' she had recently read: how commercial cab service providers track how much charge is remaining in a phone's battery when someone is using it to book a cab. If the battery is low, especially after dark, then the fare charged is automatically higher than usual. It perhaps also depends on if it's a man or a woman booking the cab, which makes it even worse because it automatically puts women in a disadvantageous position.

Karno tried to not believe her at first, but soon they were both trying to brush off the thought that there were entities out there in the world trying to convert human fear and safety into profits.

Karno said he had read about a restaurant in Japan run entirely by androids, from taking orders to cooking the food and serving it to their customers. Apparently, if one allows it, then every android waiter can read your pulse and suggest the ideal dish for you from the menu based on your health conditions.

'It's like an electric current from the android enters your body and traverses it, gathering all the information it needs, and travels back into the android's system. Who is to say it isn't carrying knowledge about your deepest fears and darkest secrets as well.'

Devaki listened carefully.

Karno continued. 'But …'

'What is it?' said Devaki.

'All our bodies are so different. I wonder how a computer chip can be right about all of us.'

'Perhaps we are not as exclusive as we think we are,' Devaki said and looked into Karno's restless eyes. He had little choice but to believe her.

5

WHAT COULD GO WRONG when your life, even if not perfect, seems to have attained the calmness of still water in an unpeopled forest?

Why do some of us crave chaos?

Why does it become irremissible then to invite a storm?

It was Devaki's twenty-first birthday that November, and she disappeared all morning only to resurface in the afternoon to tell Faiza, over a phone call, that she wanted to spend the evening only with her. But Faiza had other plans. She had never surprised anybody in her entire life, and she wanted to change that by throwing her girl a little party. Not too many people were to be on the guest list though – only a couple of Devaki's friends whose names she sometimes mentioned in passing.

Meera worked in an IT firm in Gurgaon and lived in the same building as Devaki. Once, Devaki had returned home drunk after a heartbreak and tripped on the stairs of their building, injuring herself. She lay on the first-floor landing, unable to move her left foot, until Meera found her and took her to the hospital. Since then, they had shared many evenings popping corks and clinking wine glasses, and discussing people who take other people's hearts for granted.

Then there was Chris, who, apart from being an old friend of hers from her Kanpur days, was studying literature in her college and was one of Faiza's students.

Devaki claimed, to Faiza's sheer amusement, that Chris had secretly always been in love with Faiza.

When Devaki came home and unlocked the door of Faiza's apartment that day – she owned a set of spare keys now – she wasn't greeted by the loud cheer of birthday merriment or a garishly decorated house with multicoloured streamers and balloons. A couple of yellow lights which hung from the ceiling lit up the place just adequately, with soft music playing in the background, and three of Devaki's favourite people stood with their glasses of red wine raised at her. Faiza picked up another filled glass from the kitchen table and walked up to her.

Handing her the glass, she whispered in her ear, 'Welcome home.'

Devaki had imagined spending a quiet evening, with her head resting on Faiza's shoulder, maybe sitting outside on the balcony and staring at starlight struggling against the grey smog that had covered all of Delhi's skies. But this wasn't too bad either, she thought. The evening must have taken some planning. A couple of phone calls had to be made, to people Faiza had never spoken to before. Devaki knew how hard it must have been for Faiza to pick up the phone and dial those numbers. She hated telephone conversations so much that she rarely even dialled Devaki's number. And yet she had made this happen. Devaki felt grateful for this day.

Meera gifted her a book and apologized for not finding the time to get it wrapped.

Devaki thanked her, appreciating the gift even more because it wasn't wrapped. A wrapping paper's life is so transitory, there solely to offer a brief moment of delight, when what's inside it – the thing that really matters – is handed over to its rightful owner. Who takes only a few seconds to tear it open, relieving it of its duty and discarding it like a body stripped of its soul, forever. The thought always bothered Devaki. It reminded her of the transitory nature of human life – her own life.

It was a copy of *The Return: Fathers, Sons and the Land in Between* by Hisham Matar; a memoir about a son who returns to Libya, his homeland, in search of his father who was abducted by Colonel Gaddafi twenty-two years ago and has since been missing. She opened a page and read a short review of the book by the then literary critic for *The New York Times*, Michiko Katutani: '[An] eloquent memoir ... at once a suspenseful detective story about a writer investigating his father's fate ... and a son's efforts to come to terms with his father's ghost, who has haunted more than half his life by his absence.'

Devaki read it and remembered all the ghosts who inhabited her life. Of their neighbour's son who fell in a well. Of a woman she saw go under a bus once, when crossing the road while talking on a mobile phone, anxiousness written all over her face, perhaps dealing with something so urgent that couldn't be delayed, alive one second and altered into a heap of flesh without life or shape the next.

And of her father, who used to be a manager in a cafeteria in Mumbai.

She had asked him to come back to Kanpur so many times, until she couldn't any more. Until that fateful day when a group of young men with grenades in their backpacks and hate in their hearts entered his cafe and sprayed fire aimlessly at everyone, like someone carelessly watering plants with a hosepipe. By the time they left, many were severely injured, and ten people had already breathed their last; her father was one of them.

A couple of years later, Devaki went back to the cafe and met a person at the reception who said he knew her father. He told her how brave her father was that day. How he helped people find hiding spots even in that chaos, how he chanted prayers but didn't abandon his place of work and escape through the window at the back, which he so easily could have done; how he took the bullets meant for a teenage girl, who made it out of there alive only because of Devaki's father. She hadn't cried when she saw what was left of her father's body at the hospital. But that day, when the receptionist told her about her father's story of courage, she wept for hours.

Her father who always used the zebra crossing to cross the road; her father who always reminded her to never invest in mutual funds because the commercials warned it's not risk-free; her father who sent self-curated gift boxes to their relatives on every Dussehra, who was scared of dogs both big and tiny, who stood between a stranger and her death without hesitation. It was as if she didn't know the man who was her father and was introduced to him for the first time. Ever since that day, his ghost had never left her side.

Chris, who had gone to the balcony to attend a phone call, came back inside and interrupted the silence in the room. 'Okay, let's play a game. It's my favourite game to play at every party.'

Devaki shook her head when she heard this and said, 'I've known you for twenty years now, Chris. I know exactly where you're going with this, and I have played this game at least a hundred times with you.'

'You might have, but these two haven't, and they certainly haven't ever with me,' Chris said spiritedly. 'I'm just going to ignore you and go ahead anyway.'

They all laughed.

Faiza said, 'Irshad.' Meera raised her glass to him.

'Okay, so basically the game is a simple question. If you were allowed to invite any three people to your dinner party – anybody at all, dead or alive – who would they be?' Chris said.

Meera raised her hand and said, 'I'll go first.'

'Let's hear it,' Chris said.

'All right.' She chugged some wine. 'First, Dilip Kumar. Because he was my mother's favourite person, not I or my brother. True story. Sometimes, she would even refer to herself in the third person and call herself Madhumati.'

'Best reason ever,' Devaki chipped in.

'Thank you,' said Meera. 'Number two would be Joan Baez. Because what's the point of a dinner party without music, right? "Diamonds and Rust" is the only song ever written which I could tirelessly listen to all night long. Even all life long.'

'Waah,' came Chris's approval.

Chris was the self-appointed DJ that evening. Somewhere in the room there was a Bluetooth speaker connected to his phone, and he wasted no time in changing the music to 'Diamonds and Rust'.

'Who'll be the third and final one?' he asked.

'That's easy …' said Meera, '… my mum. She left way too early, you know. One evening isn't enough with her, but it will still be something. We will eat, chat and sing together. Then I shall – like a good daughter must – take Joan and go out for a walk, leaving the two lovebirds, maa and Yusuf Sahab, alone for a while. Isn't this a perfect plan?'

Devaki high-fived Meera, and there was a wide smile on Faiza's face. Devaki couldn't remember seeing such a broad smile on Faiza's face before. Chris tried to raise an objection briefly, saying that naming family members was not allowed in the game. But Meera shut him down immediately by countering that he should have mentioned it before the game had begun.

'Okay, but whoever goes next can't do that any more. Rules are rules,' said Chris.

'Relax,' said Faiza. 'Even if you paid me, I wouldn't pick any of my family members for a fantasy dinner party. Unless it isn't a fantasy and is meant to be a nightmare.'

This caustic side of her personality was Devaki's favourite. Faiza was a woman with jagged edges, and one was meant to tread with caution and care around her.

'My first guest at any party would always be James Baldwin. If you asked me to hypothetically go out on a date with someone, a concept I wholeheartedly despise, I would still happily go out with Baldwin. When I'm dying, when a person's whole life is supposed to flash before them, then know that the last face I see before closing my eyes would be Baldwin's. He has rescued me on days when I didn't think I could be saved.'

She closed her eyes as she spoke.

'I would want him in that party for his words, of course. But mainly so my sweaty palms can be in his, so he can hold me in his arms for as long as I want. Maybe we will dance – I will rest my head on his chest as he recites "The giver" in my ears, such that no one else in the room would hear what he is saying:

If the hope of giving
is to love the living,
the giver risks madness
in the act of giving.

That beautiful, mad bastard.'

It made Devaki wonder if Faiza ever spoke of her in the same way, as she was about a man whom she remembered fondly every day. The comparison was unfair, she knew. They had only properly known each other for a few months, while Baldwin must have stayed with her through her sorrows and her rage for years. But every month has thirty days, sometimes thirty-one, and every day has twenty-four hours, and each of those hours has sixty minutes, and beyond that her interest in mathematics fades. But you get the drift.

Number two and three on her guest list came and went without much fanfare. Or maybe Faiza was tired of explaining to the world why she desired the company of someone. Just as she would hate explaining to anyone about Devaki's role in her life – the reason why they never spoke about their relationship with others, until that evening. Never before were other people welcomed into their private space, which is why that evening had surprised Devaki but also filled her with confidence. For the first time she had dared to think that maybe there was more to this familiarity, that a sense of permanence was now within arm's reach.

The only permanent truth under the sun, however, is that everything about human life is impermanent.

No one in the room noticed when envy entered through the window grille and made itself comfortable in a corner.

Devaki knew the game well. It wasn't meant to be family, as Chris had earlier announced, or friends, or lovers, or allies. Just three familiar names, people who enjoyed considerable celebrity and were comfortably out of reach. Or were fictional.

And yet she had hoped against hope that Faiza would allow her a seat at that make-believe dinner table. She didn't want to be a movie star, or a songwriter to win her place in that imaginary room inside Faiza's head. She didn't want to *deserve* a spot there but to be gifted one. Merely for existing, for being this unique concoction of atoms and molecules, grief and hope, and scars that had started resembling birthmarks. For things that were imperfect in her – things that made her *her*. Someone Faiza couldn't do without, someone indispensable to her entire being.

When a dream breaks in a concrete forest, it makes a sound which only other recently broken dreams can hear.

'Let's take a picture,' Devaki said raising her left arm, her phone in her hand. 'Let's immortalize a night which I wouldn't trade even for a fictitious rendezvous with the rich and the famous.'

Faiza was lighting a cigarette, but the clever little jibe didn't escape her.

'You two are indispensable in my life,' Devaki said to Meera and Chris. 'And Faiza … she's like my lighthouse, my personal hero.'

'Oh, she's my hero too,' Chris said.

Then Chris – the Malayali boy whose parents lived in Kochi, who grew up far away from them in Kanpur with his grandparents because his father, a blue-collar worker, and housewife mother couldn't bear the expenses of raising a child – went ahead and spoke about his admiration and adoration for Faiza.

'Have you seen her at the campus? It's like she owns the place,' he gushed.

Faiza smirked. Meera sat up. Devaki looked away.

'But not in a feudal way; more like an artist who owns a gallery during an exhibition or how a fisherman owns the sea.'

Faiza was so pleased to hear this that she returned the compliment with a nod and said, 'And you, dear Chris, are one of the brightest and sharpest minds in your class. I hope you know that already.'

Devaki couldn't resist any more and intervened to say, 'Interesting. I have never heard you say such flowery things about me. Where have I fallen short?' She scoffed.

'That's because you never let me think it and say it organically. You always ask,' Faiza said.

Devaki didn't think Faiza would respond to her question. She thought Faiza would brush it off like another minor insult. But to her surprise, Faiza didn't want to let it pass this time.

'What do you mean?' Devaki said.

'I mean that you always ask me to say something nice about you,' Faiza said without pausing, as if she had the answer prepared; as if she had been waiting to say it for a long time. 'Who can conjure up "something nice" on demand? My mind is not a video library, is it?' The words came at her with a kind of urgency, like someone who has suddenly sprung up from her bed to take care of the dirty utensils she had allowed to sit in the kitchen sink for days.

If Devaki was hurt, she didn't let it show.

She kept her glass on a windowsill and said, 'It's all right. There's no need to get irked. Sorry that I seek your approval. I didn't know it bothered you so much. Of course, I am never going to again.'

'Your only response to any sort of criticism is getting defensive,' Faiza said. 'What do you have to be so dramatic about? Why do you have to say such a thing as "I'm never going to again"? Just because someone with more knowledge and perception has called you out, doesn't mean you'll go on a self-loathing trip. This is your problem, or perhaps it's a problem with all young people.'

Human patience anyway survives on borrowed time. Faiza's words had nudged it dangerously close to the edge for Devaki.

'Well, I'm only stating the truth,' Devaki said. 'Besides, if you have issues with how "young people" are …' she said, making air quotes with her fingers, '… why are you hanging out with us right now? From what I can see, you're the odd one out here.'

Devaki could fathom the futility of the statement even as she was saying it. They were all at Faiza's house. If anyone had to leave, it was them and not her. And yet the words swarmed out of her and settled in the already heavy air of the room.

No one said anything for a few minutes.

The only sound that remained was that of the occasional sip that Faiza took of her drink.

Soon Meera got up and said she had to leave. Devaki offered to walk her to the cab.

The two friends walked down the stairs of the ageing building in total silence and waited by the road for the taxi, which was seven minutes away according to the app on Meera's phone. Devaki felt partly responsible for souring the mood of the party and felt like apologizing to her, but Meera spoke before she could.

'What are you doing, Devaki?' she asked with concern in her voice.

'What am I doing where?' Devaki said.

'This,' Meera said. 'Whatever this is you've gotten yourself into, whatever it was that was happening upstairs ... I mean ... isn't she much older than you? Do you think this is appropriate in any way?'

Sometimes the most obvious things need to be pointed out for one to take note of them. The oddness of Devaki and Faiza's equation was there for both Chris and Meera to witness that evening. Like plaster on a wall coming undone from a gust of wind, their figmental cover was blown in that instant.

'She's just about a decade older than I am,' Devaki said. 'My grandfather was fourteen years older than my grandmother, and she was younger than me when they got married.'

'Forget her age. She also teaches at your college. Can't you see how messed up this is?'

'Yes, but I don't take her classes. Chris does.'

Meera shook her head regretfully and said, 'Are you even listening to yourself right now?'

She was. It wasn't easy for her to believe that they were her own words she was hearing.

While wanting to become someone who could fit into Faiza's well-defined reality, had Devaki unknowingly beckoned her own unbecoming?

The question in front of her wasn't untimely, somewhat unexpected but not inopportune. It could have chosen to face her at a later date, or perhaps even earlier, but it chose that day. Her birthday.

Was it a sign of things to come? Was she supposed to know the answer? Was that knowledge supposed to set her free? How many times are we born in a lifetime? Once out of the womb, yes. But every time we learn something new about ourselves that changes the way we think and look at life, aren't we reborn?

Was it time then? For her to be reborn on the day of her birth anniversary?

Devaki could have made life simpler for herself by wanting someone closer to her age. It wasn't that she hadn't loved before. She had. But each time it had felt transitory, not like building a new home but rather pitching a makeshift tent next to a tidal river – waiting for the tide to rise before moving away.

Movement, she knew, was inevitable in relationships. Because we are all migrants in the economy of hearts. All of us once found a home in people we don't belong with any more. We all migrate.

6

HAVE YOU EVER SEEN a ghost? It is commonly believed that most people, who say they have, actually haven't. It's unlikely that you are ever going to meet a person who could minutely describe the feeling of being in the presence of a ghost. Perhaps it is the absence of even a sign of one that we fear more than we fear seeing a ghost. The possibility that there may or may not be a ghost in the room you are in, that's what makes our heartbeats gain momentum. When you don't know what it wants from you or what it is already making you do, or if it is even there at all. Hence, almost every ghost story we tell each other from our experience of the paranormal, mostly lacking any evidence, is a Schrodinger's ghost story.

Love often feels like that ghost.

Of all the stories about herself that Devaki could have shared with Karno, she chose this one. They took walks, they sat in churches, they visited galleries, they shared sandwiches, and they started spending a lot of time doing nothing at Karno's place. Karno often talked about his self-doubts and the uncertainties about where his life was headed. Devaki mostly spoke about the things which bothered her – the missing Oxford comma in newspaper articles; rabid Hindutva politics, far removed from the true ideals of Hinduism, slowly taking over their country; the billionaire capitalists getting richer, and the poor getting poorer. But she seldom talked about herself, and if she did, she always went back to recounting the time she had spent with Faiza, that too in snippets, mostly. But not once mentioning what happened that night after her heated exchange with Faiza … never letting him in on how their story ended. Or if it did at all.

He, of course, wanted to know the rest of it. All of it.

Karno was often anxious, behaving adamantly each time she refused to tell him more. But each time a fire started to run riot in his pulmonary valve, her fragile and stoic face would serve him ice. She also knew that he had nowhere else to go, so she had made him an offer. Instead of asking another question, he could ask her to do something for him … anything … and she would have to oblige.

'Did she need choices?' he had asked.

'No,' she had answered. She wanted to make Karno happy.

They were at his place, on his six feet by four-and-a-half feet bed – an odd size that he got made long before meeting Devaki; it was big for one person but when two people slept on it, they had to lie really close to each other.

'Come with me to the mountains,' he said.

She laughed like a child and asked, 'Which one?'

'Any, it doesn't matter which one when you are by my side.'

To which she said, 'You are speaking like you are my lover.'

He kept quiet.

He knew he didn't have the luxury to call himself her lover yet, but he also didn't know what else to call himself. He had no idea how else to be around her, if not by caring for her, paying attention to her … loving her. Karno was like that novel – neither fully literary nor devotedly commercial – lost somewhere in the midlist.

All he wished for was to spend more time with Devaki. As long as she agreed to come with him, he didn't care much about the hurtful words she unknowingly uttered.

They got on a bus the next day.

For the next three nights, they were enfolded in the mist and chill of Landour.

On the second morning, they saw that a tree facing the balcony of their bed and breakfast was being cut. It wasn't being cut down entirely. Just its green was being removed with surgical precision, all the leaves chopped off carefully, leaving behind a host of bare, patchy branches. Devaki felt helpless as she watched the tree turn into bare bones and decided to go downstairs and investigate.

From the balcony, Karno could see Devaki argue animatedly with the workers who were entrusted with the job. It was one of his favourite things to do, watching her from a distance. She was so committed towards every word she spoke, so eager about life's little idiosyncrasies, that it managed to fill him up with renewed hope each time he saw her in action.

That afternoon when they were walking towards Doma's Inn, next to which is the writer Ruskin Bond's residence, he asked her, 'Are you still upset about the tree?' Karno knew by then that these were the things that affected her more than everyday troubles.

'I guess not,' she replied. 'It was done for the people who live on the ground and the first floor, who don't get as much sun as those who live above them. And I did notice how awfully cold it gets here after sunset. If I remained upset about the incident, that would mean I am okay with this inequality. But everyone has a right to the sun … everyone has a right to warmth.'

Like always, she had managed to rationalize a hurt. Karno heaved a sigh of relief and at the same time wished in his heart to inherit this ability from her.

To move on from the subject, he said, 'We are walking aimlessly.'

'You don't like it?'

'No, I do. But it also reminds me of something.'

'What?'

'*Before Sunrise*. The Linklater film with Hawke and Delpy,' he said.

An involuntary chuckle escaped her lips.

'What?' He smiled. 'You don't like that movie?'

'I did when I first watched it. That was when I was sixteen or something. But now if you show it to me, I don't know if I'll be able to enjoy it as much.'

'Why not?' he questioned with marked disappointment in his voice.

'Where is the relatability factor, sir?' she said sharply. 'Let's face it … can any woman in India really walk around a deserted city all night without feeling unsafe every minute? Forget that, will any woman in India dare to get off a train with a stranger just because he has been charming for like twenty minutes? This is only possible in Europe. If Linklater had to make this film in India, it wouldn't be a trilogy. At most, it would be a short documentary about women's safety.'

They both laughed.

'You know, I read somewhere that all the dialogues in the film were improvised. Nothing was on paper. The two actors and the director wrote them as they went along. Isn't that beautiful? The ambiguity of not knowing where two people are headed, even in fiction?' he said.

Devaki said nothing, only looked at him to smile and then took an unexpected left turn where the road bent and entered a house. Before Karno could ask anything, she was already halfway up the stairs of that building.

What are you doing? His eyes seemed to ask.

'Come with me, this is where Ruskin lives.'

When they knocked on the blue-grey wooden door, a middle-aged man in a T-shirt and pyjama opened it. She asked for Ruskin, and the man asked them who they were. Before Devaki could make something up, Karno answered, 'I was an editor on one of his more recent books, just dropping by to say hello.'

She looked at him with mild amazement and doubt; Karno tilted his head to imply that it was true.

The man welcomed them inside.

A Labrador Retriever, the colour of liquid chocolate, walked up to them and sat by Karno's foot as they took their seats.

'He is not one of Mr Bond's,' the man said, 'but he comes exactly around this time to see him.'

Karno smiled. 'Maybe he is his favourite writer too.'

'Does he come every day?' Devaki asked.

'On most days,' the man replied. 'But especially when Mr Bond is unwell. He has named him Rambo.'

Devaki moved her eyes away from the Labrador and towards the man. 'Oh, so … he is …?'

'Not keeping too well, yes,' the man said. 'I am afraid you won't be able to meet him today.'

She looked dejected. But didn't want to be a bother for one of her favourite literary men either.

Karno's left hand was gently rubbing the dog's ears; he kept his right hand on hers.

The man then offered them tea, but Karno and Devaki were in no mood to waste any more time indoors when the hills outside were alive and calling them, so they politely refused and got up to leave.

Rambo followed their steps and came outside with them.

As they made their way downhill, in the late afternoon light, to the town of Mussoorie, Rambo stayed loyally by their side. Both Devaki and Rambo wore glum faces throughout the journey, which entertained Karno immensely. But he didn't say anything. Why irk the already distraught, he thought.

Rambo stayed by their side until they reached the Cambridge Book Depot on Mall Road.

Devaki picked up a signed copy of *The Room on the Roof*. When Karno saw her paying for it at the counter, he asked, 'Don't you already have a copy of this?'

'I do.'

'Then?'

'I wanted to own a signed copy. I haven't read him in years, but his words have kept me rooted to a huge part of my childhood. So I want to own a minuscule part of him.'

Karno smiled and told her they could always come back a few months later and try to see him again or wait for him to come to Delhi. To which Devaki replied, 'I don't think I will ever get to see him. This was my only chance.'

Karno looked at her questioningly and said, 'Why do you think so?'

Even though she had heard him clearly, she didn't say anything.

The next day, with a little bit of defeat in their hearts, they returned to New Delhi.

7

THE MORNING AFTER THEY were back from the mountains, Karno was woken up by a sudden sharp knock on the main door. Devaki was sleeping peacefully next to him, unmoved by the noise. It was possible that whoever was outside had tried ringing the doorbell first. But that thing had been out of order for a while. Except Devaki, rarely did anyone visit him, so he hadn't bothered to get it repaired.

When he opened the door, there was a man in a poorly tailored suit standing outside, while another man and a woman, wearing a uniform of some kind and a cap, stood two steps behind him. His suit was the colour of coffee; their uniform a sickly pink that resembled the colour of a cough syrup Karno used to have while growing up in Calcutta. Their faces looked composed, carrying a hint of a smile. It made him wonder if he was still asleep and this was the beginning of a nightmare.

'Good morning, did I wake you?' the man in the ugly suit asked.

Karno was visibly confused. But politeness is a virtue Indians don't forsake even when they have been untimely woken up from their sleep. Karno checked the time on his mobile phone. It was 6 a.m. He was not a morning person. He was not even a late morning person; he preferred his days to begin after noon. But he said, 'No … it is not a problem. Can I help you?'

'You certainly can,' the suit said. 'We have come to collect our package.'

Karno turned around to take a quick look inside the house to see if there was any parcel-like thing lying around. Had Devaki asked them to come and pick up something? But why would she tell them to come at this ungodly hour? That was unlikely, he thought. Then who were these people?

'I am sorry, but what kind of package are you looking for? And who did you speak to before coming here? Was it Devaki?'

The smug smile on the suit's face broadened slightly. He turned to look at his companions who smiled back at him like they were all privy to some secret. The suit swiftly checked his wristwatch and seemed lost in some thought for a couple of seconds. Then he looked at Karno and said, 'The date is correct. Maybe we came a bit early. Usually, clients remember by this time. Perhaps you have a lot going on in your mind already, and it hasn't come back yet. We have multiple packages to collect today, and we thought why not start early so we can deliver the packages to the branch office by afternoon and have the evening free to ourselves. It is a Saturday, after all.' And the three of them began to laugh.

Karno was getting annoyed now.

The suit continued, 'If you want, we can come back later, around nine. You will remember by then. Even if not everything, then enough to let us come inside and take our package back. But if you don't mind, we can collect it now, and that way we won't have to come back later. It must already be dormant by now. It is unlikely that the package will be of any use to you either.'

Karno wasn't the kind to get agitated easily, but he could feel his frustration increase with each passing second.

Did you come to my house at six in the morning to engage me in a brain-teaser contest, he wanted to ask. But he continued to show remarkable restraint and waited for his uninvited guests to solve the mystery for him.

'My name is Mr Brown,' the man said. That explained the suit colour. 'These are my assistants, Pinki and Pinku.'

Karno looked at the pair. 'Really? That is what their names are?'

'That is rather rude,' Mr Brown said. 'Why? Do you have a problem with their names?'

Karno was startled by his tone but regained his composure quickly and said, 'No, I mean … they are wearing pink uniforms and pink caps … and you're saying they have identical names … it sounds a little fishy, won't you agree?'

Mr Brown was quiet for a second and then burst into a very loud cackle that could have reached even the seventh circle of Dante's hell. 'You are right,' he said. 'It does sound strange when you put it like that. The thing is, we are not very comfortable disclosing our real names. I have renamed the three of us based on the colour of our clothes, as is fairly obvious. This is my team. FIND A FRIEND has hundreds of such teams spread all over the world. But if you ever enquire, you'll find out that there is only one Mr Brown, one Pinki and one Pinku in the entire organization. These names may be false, but they're totally exclusive.'

Karno was trying to follow everything that the man was saying as closely as he could at six in the morning.

'I still don't understand—'

The man interrupted him mid-sentence and said, 'Okay, why don't you do something? Why don't you go inside and try waking …' Then he checked something on the tablet he had been holding all this while in his left hand and continued, '… Ms Devaki? Correct? Why don't you try waking her up? And then we can talk again. We shall wait here. Maybe she did call us. We can only be sure once she's here, right?' There was an unmistakable sarcasm in his voice.

Karno waited for a few seconds, then hesitantly closed the door behind him – without locking it because he knew that he would need to be back soon – and walked inside towards the bedroom where Devaki was still asleep.

Inside, she was comfortably tucked in a blanket, her hair messy, and her face turned towards the spot from where Karno had got up just moments ago, as if waiting for his return – a sight he now lived for. He didn't want to disturb the scene. When he was a young boy, all his friends liked to toss pebbles in a pond in their neighbourhood to see the ripples take shape. Karno always liked the water more when it was still. The awareness that it could flow and travel miles within minutes and yet chose to remain in a state of tranquillity moved him deeply.

Devaki looked like the still, familiar water in that moment.

He thought of letting her sleep; she had a headache all day whenever she didn't get enough sleep. But then he remembered Mr Brown's words, and a sense of nausea mixed with fear gripped him instantaneously.

Slowly, he stepped towards her side of the bed and called her name.

There was no response.

She was a heavy sleeper. Even slept through alarms sometimes, especially when she'd gone to bed after an exhausting day.

There was a poster right above her side of the bed, hung from the wall. It was a still from Wong Kar-Wai's *In the Mood for Love*. Painted in a hue of red, it showed a woman sitting on a bed, wearing a knee-length dress, which starts where her face ends and neck begins. She is holding a glass-like object in both her hands, the fingers of her left hand holding it firmly but her right hand only barely touching its side. The bed is covered with a rose-coloured bedspread, there are two photo frames hanging on the wall of the room behind her, and she is sitting next to a bedside table which has a lamp that is on but its light not completely visible. A man's reflection is visible on a mirror that occupies the left half of the frame; he is sitting with his arms crossed, and a cigarette dangles between the fingers of his right hand.

She is staring longingly at the floor. He is looking at her.

Karno had forgotten when exactly in the film this scene happens. He had looked at the still every day since he got it framed and put it up, and yet he had never noticed its details the way he was seeing it now. A fleeting moment of romantic longing.

Karno looked towards his left. Outside his window the world was passing him by rapidly, one car at a time. Even with Devaki in the room with him, Karno felt the loneliest he had in years. He wanted to find a way out of there; he wished for an invisible tunnel that would lead him straight on to the road and inside one of those passing vehicles, that would make his life dissolve into tiny pieces as he became a part of someone else's life.

He felt embarrassed thinking about his aloneness.

Karno said Devaki's name again. This time a little more loudly. And then once again. And again. Each time his voice went up a few decibels. But Devaki didn't move.

He felt inadequate for a brief second.

Was the sound of his voice not reaching her? They were fine the evening before; did they get pulled so far apart in just one night that she couldn't hear him any more? Karno touched her arm now to shake her awake from her slumber. But as soon as his fingers touched her skin, he knew she was far gone. Her body was cold as ice. Karno had touched a lifeless body once, that of his grandfather, so he knew corpses go stony. But this wasn't the same kind of cold. This wasn't skin and flesh ready for decaying. This felt like machinery. How the aluminium body of a car parked by the road feels, the morning after it has rained in Delhi.

He tried picking her up, but it seemed as if her body had gained three times her previous weight overnight and was now unmovable. After struggling for a couple of minutes, he gave up. Karno's mind was a melting pot of confusion and delirium suddenly.

He walked back to the door, already half ajar in anticipation of his return. Mr Brown had a sympathetic look in his eyes when Karno opened the door wide and moved aside, indicating to him and his companions to come inside. Pinki and Pinku had already unfolded a stretcher which they were now carrying together cautiously, ensuring its corners didn't hit the walls or the furniture and damage anything in a house which was already about to suffer an irreparable loss.

Karno watched them raise Devaki's inanimate figure with practised hands and keep it on the stretcher. They laid her down on her back, straightened her legs and rearranged her arms, which now hung down at her sides, turned her palms so they were now facing upward. Devaki in anatomical position. Ready to depart.

'I … don't understand …' Karno managed to say with some hesitancy.

Mr Brown kept his hand on Karno's shoulder and pointed towards a wooden chair that stood next to the bed.

He did as instructed. Mr Brown sat on the bed, where moments ago Devaki was asleep … or dead. Dead? Was she dead? How could a person go to bed in perfect health and not wake up? That too someone as young as her? How could he not know when he was sleeping right next to her? How did these people come to know before even he did? Who were these people anyway?

'I feel ya … Mr Karno,' Mr Brown said.

Karno gazed at him in absolute bewilderment.

'Isn't that how young people talk these days?' he said. 'My son says that since I have to deal with a lot of young people in my line of work and often console them, I should learn to speak their language. Helps me connect better with them. I try.'

'Is she dead?' Karno asked.

'Lemme get to the point straightaway, Mr Karno,' he continued, visibly satisfied with himself. 'She is, and she isn't. You can say it's a little bit of both.'

Ironic how it held true for almost everyone, Karno thought. Who here isn't a little dead and a little alive at once – oscillating between existing and fading in a struggle for survival?

'I shall explain,' Mr Brown said.

What he said next sounded less like real life and more like a science fiction novel.

'You've known Sample 5411 …' he stopped, apologized, looked something up on his mobile phone and said, '… Ms Devaki … for the past six months, right?'

Karno nodded his head like an obedient student.

'Very well. And here, I must pause and inform you that you came to meet us exactly a week before that.'

Karno's face, as the popular Bengali idiom goes, was gradually taking the shape of the numeral five as it is written in Bangla – ৫. But one of his strengths was that he was a patient listener.

'Currently you don't remember it, and that's because of a serum which we have injected in your system. It's a compound which our company has funded and developed over several years and has patented, and before you start panicking, let me assure you it's a hundred per cent safe and is neither a physical nor a mental health hazard for our clients. That being you, in this case.'

Karno's eyes fell on the mirror hanging on the north-west wall of the bedroom, and he noticed how ugly he looked. Unkempt, cluttered and unattractive. Even if Devaki woke up from her slumber, chances were she would never fall in love with him. Or maybe she would think otherwise. It could have been that just before she went to bed that night, she had decided that she would wake up the next morning and tell him that she too wanted him as much as he desired her. He had never told her that, not in so many words, certainly. But there was no way she didn't already know it.

Mr Brown said, 'You can wait for it all to start coming back to you, which should happen in the next five or six hours. Or you can always come with us to our head office in Paharganj. But Sample 5411 has to be sent to the warehouse. I can take you through it once more as our relationship manager must have done on the day you first visited. But the simplest way to do this is to sit in the comfort of your home and go through our website. Every piece of information you need is already on that page.'

Every piece? Was he sure? Karno thought.

'I would suggest you stay at home, Mr Karno. Whatever is yours is here, even your memories with Sample 5411. There's nothing more for you elsewhere.'

8

FIND A FRIEND

What is this place? Like a club for lonely hearts? Where all the abandoned people of the world gather every week to remind each other that they are not alone. Eat, speak, sing – like a temporary hour of rain on a land that has been barren for days. Being together in their solitariness.

But then it should have been called MEET A FRIEND. It says 'find' because they are going to help you discover a companion once you sign up for it.

You walk into the FIND A FRIEND office and meet the receptionist first, like in any other office. They ask you your name and if you booked an appointment with one of their specialists before coming. You most likely did. It's a simple three-step procedure on their app. You share your booking ID with them. They thank you with a smile which everyone who has walked in before you and everyone who will walk in after you has been and will be the recipient of. They enter the ID on a screen in front of them to confirm, then point towards a solid hardwood futon with armrests and ask you to take a seat. A minute later, you are told that a relationship manager will be with you shortly. For a second you are confused and wondering if you've come to a bank.

When he meets you, he has the same smile on his face as the receptionist. They are two different people with different physiques, hair and skin, and yet they look alike. You look around the office and see employees busy at their desks, and when one of them meets your eyes, you find they all look identical too. The guy who is distributing the tea, the girl who is in front of the photocopier, the men and women who are gathered near the water cooler, all indistinguishable from one another. As if they were manufactured together in a sweatshop in China.

He leads you to a matchbox-shaped cabin, which resembles several other cabins that are on both sides of it. He asks you to take a seat and offers you a glass of water followed by a glass of wine. It doesn't seem like any other office any more. Suddenly there's no tension in the room; your shoulders relax, his smile broadens and the air around you lightens. All thanks to the glass of wine. Human comfort comes cheap.

And then, without wasting another minute, he begins.

Sitting across from you, he pushes a red button, and the wall of his cabin behind his chair turns into a gigantic screen. Questions begin to appear on it one after another, without pausing for your responses.

Do you find it hard to make new friends?

Do you feel misunderstood by everyone?

Do you think about death a lot?

Are you lonely and depressed?

Do you get nightmares?

The whole thing makes you feel like you are part of some cheap TV ad.

'You don't necessarily have to answer any of these questions if you don't want to,' the man tells you. 'We can straightaway jump to your requirement, and you can just tell me what kind of a FRIEND you are looking for.'

You don't know what he is asking. Can anyone ever answer this question with certainty?

He comprehends your hesitation immediately. This is a part of his job: reading faces.

'Don't worry, sir,' he says. 'I will take you through it.'

You realize you are already on an unknown path where you would need a guide to move forward, and this guy seems like your best bet.

'Can you please quickly answer some much simpler questions for me.'

You nod.

'These are queries regarding the FRIEND we would be finding for you, so please answer accordingly.'

You nod again.

'Gender preference? Male or female or other?'

'Female.'

'Right! Age? Say, between 25 and 30? Does that sound all right?'

You nod again.

'Perfect. Any preference on nationality?'

You tell him you don't have any preference.

'Okay,' he says, noting it down on his system, while casually mentioning that their conversation is also being recorded. 'I will just put this as Indian – will be easier to locate then.' He smiles.

'Proclivity towards any specific region?'

You shake your head.

'You are making my life easier,' he says to you.

This time you smile, but it's nothing like the kind that was on his face moments ago.

'Now let me guess,' he continues. 'You want this to be a solid, serious, intimate and passionate encounter. Not a casual escapade or a one-night stand. Am I right?'

You agree with everything he says, because he's saying everything with so much conviction.

'Now remember,' he tells you. 'All of our samples are assigned a distinct backstory. That is exactly what makes the experiences of our clients so unique and exclusive.'

You can't deny that you're mildly impressed at this point. A humanoid with a backstory? What else could make it seem any more authentic?

'So how does this work? Is there a team of writers sitting in a room somewhere in Switzerland drafting these stories? Is there a computer program which randomly selects certain characteristics and traits and allocates them to each humanoid?'

For the first time you have queries. 'Where do these come from, these backstories?'

For the first time the man looks you in the eye without flashing a smile. It weirdly disconcerts you. You hope he will look away soon because you are unable to. Soon after, his eyes light up as he says, 'I was hoping you'd ask that, sir. At FIND A FRIEND, *we like to be as transparent as possible with our clients. And not every subject can be broached in the agreement, which we'll be signing later, once we've found you your match.'*

You wait for him to disclose further information.

'These distinctive backgrounds,' he continues, 'are not created by a computer program or some screenplay writer from Hollywood.' He laughs.

'Then?'

'These stories belong to real people. People who lived these lives and had these experiences. Well, at least a significant part of them.'

You don't wait for him to say anything more and ask: 'Then why are they allowing you to use them in your samples? Please don't tell me you are stealing their data.'

'Calm down, sir,' your companion tells you. The identifiable smile is back. He raises his hand which is supposed to reassure you. 'We do no such thing. Neither do we partake in any other activity that could be against the law. You can rest assured about that.'

You wait for him to continue. He doesn't disappoint.

'You will be surprised to know,' he continues, 'how many people want to surrender their whole identities to us to start afresh. For a new chance at life. And there's no better way today, I can guarantee, than to surrender them to the FAF *servers, which only ask for some necessary factual details concerning your identity. The system then performs a few random checks to ensure that the data being supplied somewhat matches your life from your digital footprints.*

'Once you clear that phase, you can, in fact, make some money from it too. The system asks for your bank details, transfers a certain amount, and that information is only accessible to the top bosses

of the company – the CEO, the CFO, et al. In short, there's no way to connect you with the said transaction unless you commit a crime in the future. The only other thing we borrow is some of your physical features to build the humanoid, to sort of resemble the individual. But not in entirety; we always want to retain some amount of ambiguity. Then the servers wait for a stipulated period of time, and only then do they assign the collected data to a specific humanoid before releasing it in the market.

'This gap from the surrender of the identity to the release of the humanoid is provided to ensure that even if the humanoid bumps into someone who knew the actual person, they are never fully sure that it is the same individual. Also, to allow the Donor to adjust into their new life more seamlessly.'

What the fuck. Karno said it in his head.

Who the fuck has given you guys the right to fucking play god? Also in his head.

In reality, the words he uttered were, 'You mean to say there are two Devakis existing simultaneously on this planet right now? One, the real Devaki … and the other, this … this robot, or whatever version of her?'

Mr Brown stayed quiet for a minute, then took a long, deep breath and said, 'Unfortunately I cannot confirm that.'

'What does it mean you cannot confirm?' Karno asked.

'Well,' the man said, 'there's a clause in the contract that our Donors sign, which specifies whether they want their humanoids to be rented out once they have moved on from their previous life, removing all traces, or …'

'Or?' Karno asked expectantly, his fingers tightly crossed.

'Or … to be released only after their death.'

'Death?' Karno's voice choked up.

'It is unfortunate, but I cannot confirm what the case is with your humanoid, Mr Karno. As I have already mentioned before,' he said, 'only our top bosses are privy to such information.'

Karno's head was spinning. And he couldn't blame himself. A few hours ago, he was sleeping next to the woman of his dreams … and now he was living through a nightmare he wouldn't wish upon even his worst enemy. Although he had never been the kind to have enemies.

Karno collected his thoughts and tried to repeat everything the man said to him in his head to make some odd sense of his situation.

The real Devaki might or might not be alive. She might have 'donated' her personal details to this company a couple of years ago, or it could be several years too – which meant, in case she was still alive, she would be much older than her humanoid version.

If she was already dead and if that's the kind of contract she had agreed to … then, of course, these guys released her humanoid version only after they learnt of her demise.

But just in case, by some twist of fate, if she was still alive, the chances of him ever finding her were negligible. She might even have a completely new identity now – who knows, perhaps a new name, a new country, a new hair colour or even a different gender.

Gone are the days when people donated their eyes or their kidneys. The world has changed. Traders are running the marketplace of our thoughts and memories now.

9

Mr Brown also couldn't confirm how much of Devaki's story … was really Devaki's story. For the most part, he presumed. But some aspects of her personality could have been borrowed from other humanoids, or from the mountainous database of their company where the lives of other people were stored away, *safely*. Karno could recall more or less everything now, starting from how he had visited the glass building that housed their office in search of a cure for his loneliness.

He enquired if it was possible for him to rent Devaki again, although he knew it was too expensive for him to afford it a second time. But Mr Brown informed him in clear terms that even if he requested her, his application would inevitably be declined. 'The company never rents out the same humanoid to the same client again.'

Apparently, they didn't have this policy in the early days, but they had to introduce this new clause a while ago after some complications arose in a couple of cases, and the company was very particular about it.

'What kind of complications?' Karno was curious to know.

'Rumour has it,' Mr Brown told him in confidence, 'that once a man rented the same humanoid some six or seven times in a row, and when it was brought back to the warehouse, some malware was detected in its motherboard. Even after formatting its system, the error couldn't be rectified. The company was forced to terminate that machine.'

'And then this new rule came into being?'

'It wasn't an isolated incident per se. Happens rarely, but not never. So, yes. It was all very sudden and strange. It's as if …'

'As if?'

'As if the humanoid wanted to go back to the man. Like it had developed some sort of … umm … for lack of a better word … attachment.'

Karno's apartment was eerily quiet now, as if all evidence of life was erased from it. Now that he knew that Deväki was nothing but an illusion – a figment of a modern techno-capitalist society's burning, hyperactive imagination – the easiest and smart thing to do, he realized, was to let go of her.

But those few weeks with her, those felt the most real … most tangible, most palpable, most human. How could he let go of that? How could he convince himself that the many moons he saw slowly melt into the morning sky with someone he thought was *his* person, were in truth seen by him all alone, with nobody by his side? That Devaki was merely a computer software, a set of predefined programs meant to serve the narrative of his life for a brief moment in time.

Now that the effect of the serum was wearing off, every little detail started coming back to Karno. Would he have done things differently had he known how miserable he would be feeling at the end? Almost certainly, he would have. What use is a futuristic drug if it cannot show you the future first before stalling your memories!

People found like-minded people more easily before, he thought, because everybody was unique in ways that weren't purely external. When a stranger rented a room and moved into your home as a paying guest, they revealed themselves at a leisurely pace, allowing you a peek into their personality each time you went knocking at their door. When music wasn't this freely available, you could know a lot about someone by the records or cassettes they owned and carried along with them. Before Instagram became a household necessity, some people spent almost all their waking hours hanging a DSLR camera around their neck, waiting for that perfect moment to capture. And from all that they saved and even those they deleted, you could get to know the person a little better.

Nowadays, everyone is watching the same films, everybody is retweeting the same art, and more people are running a poetry page online than those who read poems. And while there's democracy in this way of life, it has also turned us into unwilling doppelgangers.

When Karno went to Intezaar Mirza's bookshop without Devaki, Intezaar Sahab noticed the vacuum next to him but chose not to ask him anything about her. Karno sat slumped in a corner, next to the shelves displaying self-help and motivational titles, burying his face in the hollow of his joined palms – how a man who breaks down mid-dua would look.

Intezaar Sahab placed a cup of tea next to Karno and said, 'Have this, and go home, son.'

Karno looked up and asked, 'Why?' Intezaar had never thought Karno's voice could sound this sharp. 'Can't I be angry at least? Can't I even sit and get a moment to myself at a place where I am the most comfortable? If you want me to leave, just say so, and I will leave right away.'

The old man said nothing, just sat down next to him.

'You know, there are elderly women in Japan who supposedly commit petty crimes only so they can get caught and find some company in prison.' The sting in Karno's voice from moments ago had faded. 'I never knew the weight of an absence could be this heavy.'

That day when Karno had first seen an ad for temporary humanoid companions was an unremarkable one, just like any other day in his life. He was taking a picture of a blooming Amaltas tree on his phone, when he had noticed the giant billboard behind it.

He could have walked ahead. *He should have walked ahead*. He should have found a way to distract himself from the storm surging inside his mind and let the thought slide away on its own. Instead, he called Sandip and asked him whether he knew these things were safe to have around or not.

Sandip yelped like someone had asked him to step on a rusty nail. 'Have you lost your mind?' he exclaimed.

They decided to meet for a drink at Sam's Cafe in Paharganj, that ancient haunt for Israelis in the city and lovelorn Romeos alike. Throughout the evening, Karno didn't say a word while Sandip kept reminding him how he was still young, why he should not rush into these decisions, while in the same breath also emphasising that he must have sex that night.

Later that evening, he took Karno to a building in the same neighbourhood, that looked like a dusty, seedy, windowless love hotel for people like him who sometimes can't find their way back home. Sandip helped him climb the steep stairs of the building, and after a few bewildering turns, they entered a claustrophobic room. Sandip made him lie down on the bed; the sheet reeked of something – sweat, semen, blood, maybe a mix of all three.

He left the room after passing on an instruction to Karno. 'Drink some water and go splash some on your face too if you can.' Karno turned his face and saw the door to the washroom was right next to the bed. There was an old Onida television on a shelf facing the bed, and a lamp on the bedside table that smeared the air inside the room with a red hue. 'I will be right back,' he said and left the room.

About ten minutes later, there was a knock on the door. Karno teetered across the floor, nearly on the brink of collapse, and reached the handle. When he opened the door, he found a young girl standing on the other side. She wore a dazzling pink top that had the word BEBE written on it and a brown skirt that didn't reach her knees.

'Sandip …?' Karno somehow managed to say.

To which she replied, 'It's just me. Rani.'

It wasn't every day that Karno hung out with people who were a lot younger than him, but he could guess she wasn't more than sixteen or seventeen years of age. Although she claimed she was twenty-two. As that absurd number came out of her mouth – who knows under what circumstances she must have had to memorize that – her eyes met his to tell him that he didn't have a choice. He had to believe her because that was her reality now.

Rani stepped inside the room and shut the door behind her with practised hands.

Karno knew he should ask her to leave, but his desire to not be alone that night outweighed any rational thought.

She didn't undress completely, only unbuttoned her skirt and came out of it. Almost as unhesitatingly, she removed her underwear too. Karno looked at the outer wall of the building where there should have been a window looking out into the vastness of the night. The girl came forward and gently pushed him on the bed, and then with utmost care took off his denims and boxer shorts. After that, she walked towards the washroom and disappeared for a minute.

On her return, she held a soaked towel in her hands, cheap polyester dipped in warm water. Then with great craftsmanship, she began to give him a sponge bath below his waist. Rani started with his toes and unhurriedly began to move upward. It lacked any sensuality and felt more like a ritual she performed before starting her work. Just how some people say a little prayer to a photograph of some god before leaving their home for work. Something she evidently did for herself, not for her subject.

Karno knew there was not going to be an opportune moment to ask her to stop. The sooner it was done the better it would be for both of them. But this feeling was new. He was so grateful to have been touched.

By the time the cloth pressed against his testicles, his penis was already so stiff that it was coming in her way as her hands meandered around his lower body. But she was unperturbed and carried on with the task at hand.

The look on her face was so industrial, her every touch so formal, that Karno soon felt humiliated by his erection. He wanted to hold her hand and run away far from there, run until they were both left with no breath in their lungs, run until the night had become day, run to a station where he could buy her a ticket to a faraway place where she could be safe and happy.

Before she had even touched his stiffness, his body trembled, and he came. Her hands stopped moving immediately after. Karno's face couldn't disguise the shame he was feeling. In a hurry, he put on his pants, and before rushing out of that room and Rani's world, he touched her arm, then in a broken, mouldy voice murmured, 'I am sorry!'

Next day, he went back to the place where he had seen the advertisement and dialled the number.

Karno picked up the phone and called the college where Devaki had supposedly met Faiza. He found friends of friends who went to that same college around the same time as Devaki might have too and asked them about a professor by the name of Faiza. He searched Facebook, Instagram, Twitter, LinkedIn and every other platform he could on the internet. But they all revealed the same thing – there was never any Faiza who taught literature, or any other subject, there. He wasn't surprised.

He boiled milk and water for two cups of coffee, then realizing his mistake made only a cup. He carried it to the edge of the balcony where the floor met the grilles and sat there putting one of his arms through a gap between the iron bars; from a distance it seemed as if his arm was suspended in thin air. He looked to his right and said cheers to Devaki, who wasn't there. The phantom coffee cup held in the phantom hand of his phantom lover greeted him back.

Karno sat there for hours, watching the night dissipating bit by bit with each passing second.

The city below him reverberated with sounds of ambulances and police vans passing by, often indistinguishable from each other, both carrying the sick inside them. From someone else's vantage point, far away from him, he would have looked like an Edward Hopper painting – a desolate, urban defeatist, awaiting the reversal of something unalterable he had just witnessed. His solitude steadily surrendering to acute disquiet.

10

AT A WATERING HOLE later that week, Karno was sipping on his fifth or sixth drink of the evening. One look at the clock would have indicated it was going to be midnight soon. There were hardly seven or eight other people in the entire place. His face was half-shaven, his hair looked unruly, and he was sporting an unironed brown shirt that clung to his chest as if putting in a plea for an embrace. An elusive hero teleported from the pages of an overrated Bengali tragedy written a hundred years ago.

Behind him, he could hear a few giggles. A group of young girls, making the most of their night out. He turned to look at them a couple of times, but his watery eyes couldn't focus on any of their faces.

One of them had had enough after a few minutes. She walked up to him and asked if she could buy him a drink. She gently touched his shoulder with her fingers when he didn't respond to her. Her touch and the faint voice that had reached Karno confirmed that she was suggesting an uncomplicated and harmless kind of flirting that most men had forgotten how to do.

Karno looked up slightly and saw her reflection on the glassy surface of the wall in front of them. She looked like the kind of woman who entered a room and won it over with her first smile alone. She was volunteering with a curiosity that he possibly didn't deserve; or maybe she wanted to know if the broken could be fixed with a few minutes of consolation.

Either way, there was not much to consider. Only a fool would have refused to participate in a moment as fluid as that one, presented to him on a shiny platter. He mumbled, 'But I am already having a drink …'

The girl had figured it wouldn't be an easy sell. She kept her calm and replied, 'Another one won't do any harm, I suppose.'

When he finally looked at her, she smiled and said, 'Finish your drink. You are not going anywhere, and neither am I.'

He should have just let her go as she headed back to her table. But he stopped her to say, 'Hey, don't you want to do something more meaningful, more vital with your life?'

'Excuse me?' she sounded more surprised than vexed.

'You're young, and pretty, and seemingly smart, and yet here you are at a seedy city bar, asking men who clearly look like they want to be left alone if you can buy them a drink. Don't you feel like using your time, this very limited time for which you're here, a little better?'

The girl shook her head but didn't lose her smile. One of her friends from her table, who had heard Karno, shouted, 'Fuck right off, dude!'

The girl walked away without saying another word.

After spending some more time at the bar, Karno realized he must head home before he passed out at the table. Or worse, on a pavement or a bench on his way back.

Once he had this dream in which he was with someone. He couldn't recall her face in the morning, but he knew it wasn't Devaki. They had even moved into a house together and shared a life, almost. In the dream, he was more cheerful around that person than he ever remembered being around anyone else. He kissed her face before leaving for work each morning. Even in his sleep he knew this was a fabricated reality that his brain had conjured up, creating an idyllic life that was both absurd and unattainable at the same time. Then one day he comes back home and tells his partner that he had quit his job a few months ago. And that he had been going to a park in the neighbourhood every day and sleeping on one of its benches for nine hours. That day he had finally decided to tell her because when he was sleeping, someone had stolen his wallet.

It was a lucid dream, in which nothing objectively terrifying happened. But, somehow, it had rattled Karno to the core.

The dream was playing like a movie inside his mind when he was on his way out of the bar, trying to steady his light-headed self on his wobbly feet. The giggles from before had now turned into full-blooded laughter. He looked at them and saw that two young boys had joined the three girls at the same table.

Karno couldn't tell which one of the three had approached him earlier. He clapped his hands to get their attention. As all of them turned towards him, he addressed the girls and said, 'So you didn't get what I was trying to tell you earlier, evidently.'

The girl sitting in the middle waved at him dismissively and said, 'Just go home, man. You're not worth it and we don't want any trouble.' He took a step forward despite having clearly heard what she had just said. When the two boys at the table noticed him getting closer to their table, they got up, and one of them extended his right hand and asked Karno to back off.

The dream, it was still vivid inside his head, and he didn't want to risk seeing it again. The recurrence of a nightmare is sometimes worse than a hard reality. He didn't know why he was still there, standing in front of five strangers much younger than him, people he had never seen before and would never see again. All he knew was that they could offer him that jolt which could help settle his tired body for the night. If you ask for something from the universe, it apparently does listen.

'Do I know you?' he took a step forward towards the guy and asked him.

'I don't think so,' the boy said.

'You are sure we haven't met or talked before?'

'I am fairly certain. Now how about you turn around and walk out of that door. We don't want to create a scene here.'

Karno touched his forehead with his hand and mockingly smiled back at the boy. 'You come here and show me your dumb fucking face and filthy attitude and then say you don't want to create a scene?' Even as the words were coming out of his mouth, Karno felt as if it was someone else speaking and not him. This was not him, this had never been him.

A feverish temptation had taken over his body, and when one of the boys said, 'What the fuck do you wan—' Karno didn't let him finish his sentence and promptly raised his voice to yell, 'I want you idiots to learn some fucking manners is what I fucking want.' Then he landed a punch on the boy's face.

It broke his nose, and the boy's face was crimson with both blood and rage.

Almost instantly they pinned Karno to the floor and started landing innumerable punches on his dreary face. It oozed blood and spit. And a sigh too if one listened closely. The bartenders working behind the bar and a few other men from other tables came rushing to stop the boys before the scuffle could get out of hand.

By then they had already ensured Karno's face would be unrecognizable to him in a mirror. One of his teeth had come loose, his nose had lost its shape; he was going to be a hideous monster hiding in plain sight for the next few days at least.

A guy who worked at the bar knew where Karno lived and was generous enough to drop him back to his place. At last, when he fell on his bed that night, his head resting on a pillow on which Devaki had laid her head numerous times, Karno could feel a sharp pain shooting up his face. But he also sensed sleep coming. Like a storm had just passed, and the skies were clearing for him another time.

11

AT A FRIEND'S WEDDING, Karno spotted a girl who he thought was Devaki and followed her to the venue's exit as she was leaving. Then he followed her home. She was driving her own car; Karno got into an autorickshaw and asked the driver to keep going behind the Honda Brio. The rickshaw driver didn't question his intentions, just said he would have to pay five hundred rupees at the end of the trip – the cheap and easy price for breaching someone's privacy.

About twenty minutes later, he watched her park the car under a tree and enter an apartment building.

He wanted to go up to her and ask her if she was Devaki or knew her in any way. But it was already quite late in the night, and he didn't want to alarm her or make her feel unsafe. So, he stayed away.

But for the next few weeks, he became her shadow. Like spring isn't far behind once winter comes, he was always in her vicinity, silently looking at her go about her day, going wherever she went but always keeping the necessary amount of distance between them, so she couldn't notice him. Near her gym, in front of her office, underneath the window of her home. At departmental stores and drug stores, at fruit sellers and florists. A silhouetted figure riding around the city and following her trail like he was deciphering a map in his hunt for hidden treasure.

She was now part of a haunting, except the spirit was yet to make its presence felt to her.

He kept hoping that she would never realize someone had been watching her. Even though nothing had happened, the mind is prone to imagining the most terrible things. More than what has happened, it is the thought of what could have happened that is more terrifying.

One day he was behind her in a park where she was walking a friend's dog, and he overheard her talking on the phone. She had just received a promotion at work and was throwing a small party at her home the following Saturday. 'Bring your friends,' she said to all of them.

Nobody met interesting people at bookstores any more. Because everybody was busy meeting people at a friend-of-a-friend's house party.

Karno waited outside her building, watching men and women who looked like they could be her age and dressed for a party, taking the elevator and going upstairs one by one. He counted till he had spotted twelve such people. That was a big enough number to go unnoticed for a little while, he thought. He waited for the guard to leave his desk which he did once every fifteen minutes. Then he walked inside the building.

He expected his heart to be racing as he rang the bell, but he felt surprisingly calm. Longing had turned him into a seasoned criminal who was demanding answers from the universe. A guy he had seen enter the building an hour ago opened the door and asked him to come in. Karno had deliberately waited until it was after ten o'clock, hoping everybody was slightly inebriated by then.

His eyes searched for her as soon as he was inside the apartment. Her name wasn't Devaki. Karno was aware of that already from all those days of shadowing her. But he wanted to make sure; see her up close and rule out every possibility.

It was a large apartment, with two bedrooms, and a large hall where most people were hanging out. There were photographs in aesthetic frames on almost every wall. Not prints of famous paintings, not posters of classic films, but photographs. Of empty, urban public spaces. Parking lots, phone booths, subways, cinemas. Desolate and monochromatic. A clear pattern. A distinct taste and coping mechanism rolled into one.

A couple of minutes later, he could hear that now-familiar voice coming from the direction of the kitchen. She was on the phone again; someone was asking for directions to her house. Maybe it had not been long since she had moved into this place. And even though he was fairly sure that this person wasn't Devaki, he was oddly glad to see her doing well in life.

'Does anybody want more kebabs?' she asked as she came out of the kitchen and into the hall.

One of her friends, a Caucasian man, said, 'No, now you come here and sit with us.'

'In a minute,' she smiled and replied.

He was not having any of it. 'Come on now, we didn't come all the way here for kebabs. Or the wine. Okay, a little bit for the wine. But we are gathered here to celebrate you tonight. And you decide to spend more time with your oven than with us!'

Giving in, she came outside with a drink in her hand to join the rest of the crew. She sat down with her back towards Karno and still didn't notice the impostor. Some pop hit from the eighties was playing on a speaker, while two women were slow dancing to it in a corner.

The doorbell kept ringing every few minutes. Sometimes a food delivery guy, a couple of times some friend's acquaintance dropping by. Karno felt a tinge of envy to see how easily people were able to find company in other people, even those they were meeting for the first time.

No one paid heed to him as he slipped inside the bedroom. On her bedside table were a pair of glasses, a hibiscus plant and a self-help book about personal growth. Devi would never read this, he thought and smirked. The most noticeable thing in the room was a shelf full of old vinyl records. He took out a few, mostly jazz records like one would expect to find in writer Haruki Murakami's home. He recognized some of the artists like Charlie Parker, Ella Fitzgerald, Nina Simone. When he put them back and turned around, there was someone at the door.

Karno knew he was moments away from being exposed. But he remained calm. His burning desire to learn the truth about Devaki had turned off some button inside him that dictated shame or guilt. It wasn't her, but another woman from the party who had seen him fiddling with records in the dark.

'Hey,' she said.

Karno nodded in return.

'I am Leela, and you are?'

'Karno …' he said in a soft voice so it wouldn't reach the next room.

'Hey, Karno. Are you here with Simon?'

He hesitated, 'No …'

'Oh, sorry, I presumed because half the people here tonight seem to have been invited by him.'

Karno didn't say anything, simply stood in the unlit corner of the room and avoided meeting her eyes.

'You don't talk much, do you?'

Karno was lost for words, out of options, and the thought of where he was and what he was doing was finally dawning upon him. Like mist clearing in front of a pilgrim on the high mountains revealing a faded sun in the distance.

'I think I should leave,' he managed to mumble. 'Excuse me.'

As he was going out of the woman's bedroom, she bumped into him. The woman smiled and immediately noticed his harrowed, crushed face. 'Hey, are you all right?' she said.

'No,' he replied.

'Come outside and sit down, please. I'll get you some water,' she said considerately.

This proximity allowed Karno to look at her more closely – the way her eyes crinkled when she spoke; the sharpness of her thin, pointed nose; her collarbones which protruded prominently. His heart may have been wandering, but it didn't require any further confirmation. The resemblance was undeniable. But most of us look like someone else; we just tend to forget that because we don't look at others carefully enough.

'I shouldn't be here,' he said to her. 'I'm sorry.'

He rushed towards the main door; the party outside had got louder. As he stepped into the corridor and began walking towards the stairs, she stood at the door and asked him, 'Do you know me?'

He turned around and looked at her for the last time. He knew he owed her an answer for what he had done. But all he could say was: 'I thought I did. I really thought I did.'

12

One of his friends had set Karno up for a date. It wasn't something new; he had a few good friends, including Rhea and Sandip, who always looked out for him.

But lately, every time they would tell a common friend or an acquaintance about Karno and get her even remotely interested in meeting him, he would turn down their offer. It was as if moving on from those few weeks of his life that he spent with Devaki wasn't even an option he could consider yet. But this time, he said yes, because his friend had mentioned that she's cute, and her Instagram page very clearly suggested that she preferred actual poetry to Instagram poetry. It was filled mostly with poems, and there were barely a couple of photographs in which one could even see her. In one, the wind was blowing through her hair and hiding her face; in another, the sun was playing cat and mouse with her features. But her one-line bio read that she hated writing poems.

Karno found it interesting; someone who loves to read poetry but hates writing it. He thought that was rare in people, to love an art form with no desire to practise it.

They met at a restaurant she had picked. It served Korean food and was close to Karno's house. He decided to walk to the place and meet her there directly. As he walked in he realized it was very dark inside the restaurant. Like a moonless night. Like someone had invited him home but forgotten to switch on the light.

'I cannot see your face,' Karno said to her. He looked at a man in a suit behind the counter and repeated, 'Why is it so dark in here? I can't see anybody's face.'

'That's okay. Let it be,' she said and giggled. 'That way you will listen to me better. Men anyway have a hard time doing that. Plus, you already know how I look.'

A waiter showed them towards a table in a corner, away from the bar counter and the men and women who were busy dancing near a French window which had no business belonging in a dimly lit restaurant like this one.

'Okay,' Karno said once they were seated. 'Where do you want to begin?'

She laughed a little and said, 'Well, you tell me. Where do *you* want to begin?'

Karno thought for a moment and, after scrambling for words, uttered, 'Why don't we start with our names?'

'You don't know my name?' she asked.

'I mean, I do,' Karno said. 'But I have never heard it from you. It would be nice to hear it from you … is that weird?'

She started saying something but stopped. She took out her phone from her purse and kept it on the table, and then continued, 'No, no. When you put it like that … it is not weird at all. My name is Suchitra.'

'Hello, Suchitra,' Karno said. 'I am Uttam.'

They both waited for a couple of seconds before breaking into laughter. An in-joke meant mostly for Bengalis.

'You asked me my name, only so you could say this … didn't you?' she said.

'I won't entirely deny that possibility,' Karno answered. 'But no, that wasn't the only reason. In fact, it was only a tiny fraction of the real reason. I just really wanted to hear your name in your own voice.'

'Why?'

He took a deep breath and said, 'Because now I know what any of those people who are in your life might have felt like when they met you for the first time. Now I am not a total stranger for you any more, at least in my head. Now I am part of that large group of people, like your friends or ex-lovers, who know you more than I do.'

Suchitra ordered two bottles of soju and asked him if he would like to get to know her better.

'Unquestionably,' Karno said.

Such an odd word to use in conversation, Suchitra thought and raised one of her eyebrows, but Karno couldn't see it.

As the evening progressed, they got increasingly drunk. 'I think I am a little drunk,' Karno said at one point. After which they ordered three more bottles of the clear, colourless liquid. One each, and then they shared the third bottle. He told her about all the things he had read that week and about all the films he planned to watch but couldn't get himself to because he was too busy staring at the ceiling. They both laughed in synchrony once again.

'If you could choose to be anybody in the world, not a famous personality, just anybody in this world … who would you be?' she asked.

Karno took less than a second to answer, 'A cowboy.'

'A cowboy? Really? On a Texan ranch or romancing on the hills like *Brokeback*?'

'It doesn't matter,' he said. 'As long as I am one.'

'Well then, cowboy, tell me an interesting thing. Anything.'

He took a few moments to think, checked if there was any more alcohol left in the glass bottle; 'Not a drop more, you drunkard,' she said, and so he went back to thinking and eventually said, 'Do you know how our moon was created?'

'I think you're going to tell me.'

'This giant body, almost the size of Mars, known as Theia, collided with the Earth, which threw these vaporized chunks of our planet's crust into outer space. And then these ejected particles came together somehow, something to do with gravity and shit, and created a moon … our moon.' Karno looked outside through the window behind Suchitra and said, 'There … that moon right there. The "chaudhvin ka chand" *moon*, "the dark side of moon" *moon*.'

She turned around and her neck looked like the slenderest thing Karno had ever seen. As if one of those interplanetary chunks which was meant to form the moon had stuck around the Earth to become a part of her instead.

'We ran as if to meet the moon,' he said.

She turned around and looked at Karno looking at her.

'Robert Frost.'

One of the waiters came and informed them that they could move to another table which was better lit, if they wished to, because one had just become empty. Karno noticed the distant moonlight brushing against Suchitra's face, just like his fingers caressed the morning dew on the grass in winters. They were all right where they were, he said.

'I am having a really good time,' she said.

Karno nodded his head like a schoolboy and said, 'I am having a really good time too, Suchitra.'

Her phone beeped and a pink light came on the screen for a second before it went dark again. She looked at it and smiled from ear to ear.

'What is it?' he asked.

'Nothing,' she said.

'A text from someone special?' he questioned. 'You can tell me. We have just met, there is nothing to lose here.'

She shook her head gently and said, 'I don't get too many texts, because I don't reply to most people. This is a new app I have downloaded on my phone.'

'What does it do?'

'If I switch it on and place the phone in such a way that my phone's camera can see me, then this app reads my face at all times. It tracks what my face is saying, tells me how I am feeling by studying my expressions. Isn't that amazing?'

Karno was both amused and befuddled at once. Have we become that disconnected generally that we don't even want to figure out for ourselves how we are feeling any more? He thought, but instead said, 'So what does that pink light indicate?'

'It implies …' Her smile broadened. '… it implies that this is the happiest I have been all day today. This is the happiest moment of my day.'

They went home together. Her home. She was happy to go with him to his house too, but he insisted they go to hers instead. He felt unusually comfortable around her. He had become so unused to that feeling, that now it unnerved him.

As they entered her apartment, he began to take off his shoes. But she stopped him and said it wasn't necessary. Maybe it was an early sign that she wanted him to leave soon, Karno thought. There was a small couch in the living room where she asked him to sit and went into what seemed like her bedroom. The wall opposite the couch was covered with so many framed pictures that it was difficult to believe there was a wall behind the frames at all. It wouldn't be so bad, Karno thought. A wall made only from memories. Too flimsy to survive an earthquake but strong enough to protect one from the harsh seasons of aloneness that big cities come with.

Three faces appeared more often than the rest in those pictures. Two of them looked like they could be her parents.

Sixty-ish, both balding, smiling, always with their arms around Suchitra. The other was a man, a little bit older than her, perhaps as old as Karno, clean-shaven and a little overdressed in every picture with his hands mostly in his pockets.

She came back and asked if she could offer him a drink. He nodded. They sat down with two glasses of ice-cold white wine, which really hurt his throat, but he didn't say anything. He was learning to complain less. Take small sips and you will be okay, he reminded himself. And not just when it came to chilled wine. That is how he had decided to approach life now. Not all at once. But in intervals.

'Nice pictures,' he said after taking the first sip.

'Thanks,' she said. 'Some of the most important people in my life are here. Mostly old friends and parents, of course. Those two,' she said pointing her finger to the balding couple.

'I figured,' he said with a smile. The uncomfortable question remained unasked, left suspended in the air for some time.

'A couple of them look a bit older than you,' he said after a pause.

She laughed and walked towards a photograph in which she and the man were standing in front of a museum in some other country. Karno guessed it was somewhere in Europe, so it was someone with whom she had travelled far and wide. But he couldn't be sure.

'You mean him?' she said. 'We clicked this one in France. It was one of the best summers of my life.'

'Umm … a boyfriend?' he asked.

'Not a … The boyfriend. I have had only one. This one. For so many years that I have forgotten how to count now.'

Suchitra saw Karno fidgeting in his seat, so she said, 'Don't worry. This was all in the past. We separated last year.

Now there is just hurt that remains. I have been meaning to take down these pictures. Nobody has visited this house in months, other than friends, I mean. Friends who know about my life. Nobody … n … n … new, I mean,' she stuttered.

'I am sorry,' he said sheepishly. 'I didn't mean to ask something too personal.'

'It isn't,' she said. 'It is just a memory now, not too real. Just something which will live and die with me but without having any ramifications in my life now or later.'

'Okay, I am glad you told me.'

'What about you? You look like someone who has loved and misplaced it too. Or have I completely missed the mark …?' she probed.

Karno looked away and tried changing the subject. 'This wine is really good. You must tell me the name before I leave.'

Suchitra said, 'It is okay if you don't want to talk about it.'

Since Devaki was *taken*, Karno hadn't spoken about her to anybody. He hadn't mentioned to anyone about what happened that dreadful morning, or six months before it. He hadn't even uttered her name since. Once the effect of the drug had worn off and he had recollected everything that had preceded that unplanned morning, it wasn't too difficult for him to put the pieces back together. He now lived in a world where anything was possible. It is both a blessing and a curse of being a part of a future that your parents would only talk about when you were still a child.

In the future, cars will fly. In the future, we will go on holidays to the moon. In the future, we will have colonies on Mars. In the future, no one will die. In the future, everyone will be rich. In the future, everyone will have food on their plate. In the future, we would be able to predict the future.

But this is as far as we have come – AI companions for rent for half a year. Just another invention by greedy corporates to make more money, or the solution to temporarily fill the hollowness of the human heart for which there is no known cure in science.

13

Karno resumed his search for Devaki by going to her campus.

There was a mammoth bronze statue of the Indian politician and Hindutva sympathizer Deendayal Upadhyaya near the entrance of the college where she had possibly met Faiza, behind the main gate. That's an odd thing to have been placed there, he thought.

He looked up at the iron signboard fixed on top of the gate and read the name out loud again.

'D … U … Memorial … College.' Aah, of course, he thought.

Entering the campus wasn't difficult for him. But getting past all the babus and begums sitting in its large offices – gathering dust since the Battle of Plassey – was too daunting a task for someone whose weakest trait was making small talk. Numerous Bollywood films of the 1970s and 1980s have taught a whole generation of people that to move even a single sheet of paper from one table to another inside a government organization, you ought to start by bribing the peon. But those days are long over. Everything has become electronic now. If your face is not well known or if you don't know someone who knows someone whose face is well known, then it is almost impossible to dig out any information from that cesspool.

He walked from one table to another several times; he sat on at least seven wooden benches and waited for someone to be back at their desk to have a word with them.

One lady informed him dispassionately that it was her lunch break less than a minute after she had returned from another break, leaving Karno wondering if he had come to the right address, after all, and that a wrong turn somewhere had not landed him at an SBI branch instead.

Admittedly, it felt incongruous to be alive in a world in which these two macrocosms existed simultaneously – a huge, bureaucratic, red tape-ridden government institution which hadn't changed at all in decades … and a radical, space-age, futuristic outfit like FIND A FRIEND which sold motorized dreams to a generation of lonely people. How many worlds are contained inside the one visible world? How many micro galaxies does it take to form one whole galaxy? How many people is one individual made of? The galaxies, the worlds, the people, like hollow Russian dolls, designed to fit inside each other. The lowest common denominator is the human heart, too distant from the sun … locked away in anonymity.

After an exhausting day, Karno left the campus empty-handed and with his thoughts even more muddled than before.

14

THERE WERE TWO WOMEN named Meera in the IT firm where Devaki's friend worked, unless that was made up too. When the polite receptionist called their extension, one of them said she knew a Devaki and asked Karno to wait downstairs for her. Karno wondered if she was willing to see him only out of curiosity. As he waited for her in the lobby of that tall building – one among many in its vicinity, each named something as indiscriminate as Millennium or Galaxy or Pinnacle, always followed by the same word: Tower; as if that was a prerequisite to secure a place in that coveted compound, to be a tower and no less in an everlasting contest of towering over each other – he was abruptly filled with mild abhorrence when he thought about what he was doing.

Was this how stalkers behaved?

Fifteen minutes later, Meera walked out of the elevator wearing a formal black suit. She was a little older than Karno had imagined; not resembling just another *anybody* who worked at an IT firm in Gurgaon but someone important, someone who had already paid her dues and risen up the ladder.

'Can I help you?' she asked.

Karno kept his hesitation aside for a second. He told her he was there for a slightly odd matter and asked if she had some time to spare. Or else, he could always come back another time.

She scrutinized him from head to toe. Wearing a loose linen shirt and a pair of denims, with his dishevelled hair and a tote bag that read 'We are all stories in the end', he looked rather harmless. Meera asked him to follow her and made her way towards the cafeteria.

The cafeteria was fairly empty, and they sat down at a table close to the counter. He assumed it was because she wanted to offer him a cup of coffee or something. But she got straight to the point and said, 'Whatever it is that you have to tell me, please keep it short. Fortunately, you've come on a Friday, otherwise I don't even have ten extra minutes to spare when I am at work.'

Karno did not know where to begin, so he went with the most obvious question. 'Do you know someone called Devaki?'

Meera had just taken her cell phone out from her jacket pocket when she heard Devaki's name and stopped. Her face lost colour, but not in the way fear makes your face lose colour. It was more of a desolate look that seemed to have consumed her instantly, and her eyes looked incredibly sad. She was lost in her thoughts for a minute or so after that and said nothing, which convinced Karno that he had made the right decision by going there.

'I am really sorry if that upset you,' he said eventually.

It worked. She broke out of the trance. Then composing herself, she spoke slowly. 'No, it's just that I haven't heard that name in a very long time.'

Karno had just begun to see a ray of light in her words when a flurry of questions set him back once again.

'How do you know Devaki? How is she doing? Where has she been all these years? Do you know where she is now?' Meera asked.

If he had a magic lamp that could grant him just one wish that very second, he would have asked for it to rewind time by a few seconds, to the exact moment when Meera had admitted that she knew Devaki, and pause it there for at least twenty-four hours. So that he could spend an entire day hoping, believing that he was getting closer to the place where he wanted to be, the place where Devaki might be.

But there was no genie in sight. He just shook his head.

'You don't know?' she said.

'I mean … I don't know where she is or how she is. I just know her,' he said. 'And I was hoping you could help me find her.'

Meera looked mildly surprised. 'But how do you know her? When did you meet her?'

'A few months ago …'

'Where?'

'Here, in Delhi.'

'When did she come back from Kanpur? Did she give you my office address?' she asked.

Karno remembered that Devaki's mother lived in Kanpur. So much of her story was proving to be true. She might have been an engine-run, lifeless machine, but the life story she narrated to him was about as faithful as his own. There was some joy to be derived from that information, he admitted to himself.

'She didn't give me your office address,' he said. 'I found it on the internet. She had spoken to me about you, had told me how you guys met and where you worked. That is how I was able to find you.' And before she could say anything, he added, 'Well … to be completely honest, I didn't actually meet her. I met someone like her. If you're not in a hurry, then I can tell you how it happened.'

Meera remembered she had a bunch of meetings planned for the afternoon, but she could tell she might have to postpone each one of them now.

'Who are you?' she said. 'Some cousin of hers?'

This broke Karno's heart into several hundred pieces. Why did she have to call him her cousin? Did he look like a cousin? He knew some people looked like cousins, some even distant cousins. Couldn't Meera think of him as an old lover of Devaki's? If Milind Soman had walked up to her and asked about Devaki, would her first guess have been that he was a cousin of hers? Surely not. Because Milind Soman doesn't look like anybody's cousin. He looks like a lover or a best friend. Karno felt bad for himself, although he couldn't exactly decide why.

'No, absolutely not,' he protested defiantly.

'Then?'

Karno took a deep breath and said, 'We met under unusual circumstances and became very close.' As soon as those words came out of his mouth, he cringed at himself.

'Wait,' she interrupted him, 'before you begin, would you like to have some tea or coffee?'

Finally.

'I wouldn't mind a cup of coffee to be honest,' he said with a thankful smile.

She ordered two americanos for them and asked him to carry on. Without wasting another minute, without fumbling for words, Karno began.

He told Meera about the thief who had accidentally made them meet; about the afternoons they had spent walking around Delhi searching for nothing in particular, the time they had spent lying lazily on the green grass carpet of the primordial Lodi Gardens, sharing life histories and inside jokes, and the many nights they had spent ruminating about the past and speculating about their future. He told Meera about taking Devaki to the bookshop where he sometimes worked, and then went on to describe how in no time she had charmed his septuagenarian friend, Intezaar Sahab. Karno sounded most cheerful when he was telling Meera about their little trip to the mountains; about finding Ruskin's house and meeting his dog, the adorable and winsome Rambo. It all came back to him in a flash.

Then came the tricky part. How does one relate something as odd as that? What could be less strange than what really happened to them? Perhaps he could tell her that Devaki went away to someplace where a war broke out and she was killed in an air strike, and it would still appear less strange than the truth. Or that a deadly virus which allegedly came from bats and spread in many countries across the globe somehow got to Devaki and she died. Or that she was on a ship which sank in the Atlantic after hitting an iceberg, or that she made a pact with the devil and sold her soul to him and was now serving eternal damnation in hell. Any of these would still sound more believable than what he was about to tell her.

'Have you heard of something called FIND A FRIEND?' he said.

'Are you trying to give me life advice?' she said.

'Umm … what? No! It's the name of an organization.'

She responded, 'No. What is it? A dating app?'

'Not exactly. As the name suggests, they literally find a friend for you. It's not by matching profiles or by helping you start a conversation with a stranger.'

'Then how is it done?' she asked inquisitively.

He told her about the humanoids, and how they were customized with a different backstory each time to fit a user's requirements and personality. He told her about the serum that made him forget the entire process of renting 'Devaki' for six whole months, which he now felt passed too quickly. In short and sparse sentences, he presented this information to Meera, ensuring that he wasn't sounding too dramatic or disturbed.

Meera listened to him deliberately, her face was attentive, her eyebrows knitted together in a frown, her lips pursed. This wasn't a world which shocked the people living in it any more. Most things they thought could never happen had already happened. Changes which were hard to understand were taking place every day. People were learning to live with only as much data as they needed to sustain themselves, because finally they had begun to realize that there was too much of it out there. Nobody said 'Data is the new oil' any more. Karno's father liked using that line a lot when Karno was growing up. It is time to replace that sentence with: 'Data is the new air.' The only way to avoid it … is by holding your breath.

None of this seemed to come as a complete surprise to Meera. She had lived long enough to learn that expecting a particular kind of present was a redundant endeavour in a world that was too used to changing quickly. And it wasn't interested any longer in knowing if people could keep up. Despite that, this new information had certainly made her restless. And she was making no effort to hide it.

Meera waited for him to finish speaking and then said, 'It's all a bit much to process. But Devaki was always the odd one out, all her life. I'm not finding it too difficult to believe that she did something as impulsive and, frankly, as dangerous and idiotic as this. It'll still take me some time to swallow this pill. But surely you didn't make the effort of finding me and coming all the way here just to tell me about her, did you? You want something from me. Tell me … is there anything that I can do for you?'

As Karno began to answer, his voice rose and fell, as it always happened whenever he tried to quieten his thoughts. He told Meera that he needed to find Devaki. Or at least know where she was, if she was at peace, and if there were people in her life who cared about her. Or if she was gone forever. He knew even if he managed to find her, she wouldn't know who he was. But that was the thing, he hadn't exactly set out in search of a person. Moreover, the one he had met was not even her. At best, she was a blurry reflection of Devaki, who resembled her from a distance but up close was someone else entirely. Karno had to complete Devaki's story in his head.

His novel had remained unfinished for years. His present was an endless, empty lane leading to nowhere. He often felt like a supporting character in his own life. That half a year had felt like his life had found an anchor; that he could be in the shadows if he wished to and there would still be someone who would hold him and tell him about what was happening in the light. Karno had made peace with the fact that she was gone from his life for good, but he didn't want her to remain a mystery, a labyrinth with no exit. There's something more here, something else to this story, his heart insisted. Only struggling writers can fall for such overindulgences. It had led him wandering to Meera's doorstep, looking for answers, or at the very least to find one missing piece of this elaborate puzzle.

15

Meera couldn't guide him to Devaki. After that night of the party, she rarely saw her. Even though they lived in the same building, Devaki had started keeping to herself. Slowly, she had stopped attending classes too. Meera knew this because she would find Devaki's balcony door open every afternoon when she left for work; when Devaki went out, she always shut that door before leaving to prevent the pigeons she so vehemently detested from entering her living room. She was a politically charged person, so in all possibility only when there was a demonstration or a rally in the campus would she turn up. As more time passed, Devaki became even more distant.

Then one day, she came to Meera and said that she was leaving. When Meera asked her if she was going home to her mother, Devaki didn't say anything. Meera could tell that Devaki was leaving for some time and that she wouldn't get to see her for a while. Meera felt she needed the break. Soon after, Devaki's cell phone became unreachable and no matter how many times Meera tried to call her, she just couldn't get through. Eventually she gave up trying, thinking that she might have lost her phone or changed her number. Or for some reason, didn't want to stay in contact with her.

When she didn't come back even after a few months, Meera called up her mother's home and found out that she had indeed returned to Kanpur after leaving Delhi. But only a month after her arrival, her mother had passed away, and a few weeks after that Devaki had left Kanpur and never went back there. She had also given up her rented apartment in Meera's building, so even if she came back to Delhi, Meera had no way of knowing unless Devaki tried to contact her – which she didn't. All of this had happened nearly ten years ago.

Karno took out his phone without wasting a minute and looked up the year of FIND A FRIEND's inception and found out they began their operations in India in 2010. They must have started small, discreetly, realizing the potential of their idea in the near Indian future. The timeline fit, more or less. Devaki must have seen this as a way out. Even if she had finished her education, with her parents gone and no one else to call her own, FAF must have seemed like an opportunity for a life of anonymity. Plus the quick cash wouldn't have hurt.

Why she did what she did was an insignificant question, and Karno understood that. Why do we do the things we do? First Faiza, then her mother – the two most important people in her life – were separated from her in such quick succession. Carrying the burden of a broken heart, perhaps she could only find respite in the idea of a fresh beginning. But even when we know we are going to be gone forever one day, we want our stories to survive. All of us die twice in a single lifetime. Once when our body perishes and our mortal remains are buried or sent to the pyre. And again, when we fade from the memory of the last living person who remembered us.

Every person's memory is a unique spaceship which stays outside our atmosphere but keeps hovering around earth, only to occasionally make its presence felt. When no one remembers the person any more, the spaceship returns to its home planet of obscurity, and with it goes the final remaining morsel of our life.

Devaki wanted to disappear but not be forgotten. That is perhaps why she left behind her story in these semi-humans, who would keep her alive in some way. Was this the first time that Devaki was brought into existence? They had said to Karno that the servers usually waited for a few years before assigning an identity to a humanoid; maybe in Devaki's case they waited longer. Or maybe she was brought to this new life before too, in some other city, meeting someone else, sharing her life's story with them. An intense bout of jealousy took over Karno's body, and he stood motionless in his place like an unfinished wax figure.

The Devaki he had met was in her mid-twenties. And if everything she told him was from nearly ten years ago, before she vanished, she would be in her mid-thirties now. But this wasn't everything that he learnt from Meera. Devaki had made a massive modification to her story before signing up with FAF. Meera, as he could now confirm, was real. Devaki's classes and the college she attended, although a different one, existed. It was also true that she had fallen frantically in love with a professor. Many of her characteristics and traits sounded familiar to Karno when Meera was telling him about her, except there was one significant alteration. The professor she was in love with, her name was not Faiza. That professor's name was Ananda. *His* name was Ananda Reza Chowdhury.

A name Karno promptly recognized. He was everything Karno wasn't. A renowned novelist, poet, teacher, who legendarily also played the harmonica at many literary events around the world, winning the affection of the press everywhere he travelled. He was not on social media, but enough was written about him periodically by both his fans and detractors. Literary awards had dried up in the past few years, and his books didn't sell as much as they used to, but that didn't act as a chink in his flourishing armour. He was revered.

He was liked and disliked by an equal number of people in the publishing world; Karno had heard so from his acquaintances in the business. He was also infamous for having a bit of a temper. In fact, Karno knew much more about Ananda Reza Chowdhury than Meera could tell him. That's because Karno had secretly wanted to be Ananda Reza Chowdhury since the time he started writing. All his essays were bookmarked and saved on Karno's computer. Ananda's was a success story which Karno wanted to emulate. But he had never understood how to go about it. Meeting Meera had indeed helped him find a piece of the puzzle. And the next one he already had with him. Karno knew where he lived.

16

KARNO WAS AWARE THAT the man went out every morning to cycle, mostly inside the gated society where he lived and sometimes to the Jawaharlal Nehru University. He had read it in a personal essay Ananda had written for an anthology of essays on everyday habits. Ananda wrote about taking a bicycle to JNU every morning, around six-thirty or seven, and sitting there until he spotted a peacock – the most interesting bird according to him – which often didn't take too long. All the guards knew him and nobody ever stopped him, even though he wasn't a member of the faculty at the university or visiting a student.

Karno religiously waited outside the exit gate of Pocket 7, Vasant Kunj, where Ananda lived, for almost a week every morning. But he was nowhere to be seen. Eventually he got fed up and decided to abort this fruitless mission. Except nobody ever gives up without a final attempt. It is one of the most inept attributes of being human. Refusal to accept failure has ruined more lives and families than failure itself. Karno had dug out a landline number which was registered under Reza's name. As a last attempt, Karno dedicated an entire day to Ananda Reza Chowdhury and decided to station himself at a tea shop right outside the gate from morning until it was time for the shop to close at night. Fortunately, he didn't have to wait that long.

At around five in the evening, Ananda stepped out of the gate, not on a bicycle but on foot, and went for a stroll.

Karno followed him for an hour, during which time he visited a medical store, took two rounds of a park, came back to the same tea stall and had a cup of sugary tea before heading back home. It was as uneventful as a fifty-five-year-old's evening walk should be. Unless the fifty-five-year-old is Shah Rukh Khan.

Later that evening, Karno called Ananda on his landline phone, hoping that he would pick up. Luckily, he did. There was really no plan in his head. He thought he would let his intellectual virtuosity handle it but couldn't tell exactly at what moment his imagination took over.

Once Ananda picked up and said hello, Karno began, 'Good evening. Please listen to me very carefully. I need to talk to you, and it's very urgent. I assure you that it won't take too long. Meet me tomorrow, for an hour or so. I'll let you know the time and place if you agree. And then we can both forget this happened and go our own ways.'

He could hear Ananda's intense breaths rise and fall on the receiver at the other end. He wondered what model of telephone it could be; Ananda looked like someone who used one of those antique black rotary dials.

Ananda waited for a few seconds and then spoke, 'I'm assuming if I say no, there'll be consequences?'

'Yes. Consequences which neither of us would particularly enjoy. I know where you live, and I also know your evening schedule, Mr Chowdhury. The park you take your walks in, the tea stall you frequent. I don't want to disturb you at a public place, but if you leave me with no other choice, I may have to.' Karno paused for a moment.

He couldn't believe these words were coming out from his mouth. But he had already started something and had no choice but to go through with it. 'You're a sensible man, and I don't mean any harm. I just have a few questions to ask, and then I'll be on my way. I hope you'll make the right decision.'

This time Ananda didn't take any time to reply. 'All right. I'll meet you and try to answer your questions. But I don't go out much and prefer cremation grounds to coffee shops or shopping malls. So why don't you do one thing. Come over to my house at six tomorrow evening. I guess you don't need my address.'

It should have raised some suspicion in Karno, but desperate times call for half-baked measures. 'Okay,' he said and hung up.

Next evening, when Karno rang his doorbell, Ananda opened the door and there was an amused look on his face. As if he was expecting someone else and was surprised to see Karno instead. Ananda was holding a kitchen knife in his right hand and was wearing a white apron on which the words 'Nice to Meat You' were printed in bold.

'Are you the one who called me yesterday?' he asked.

Was he smiling? It was hard to tell. The lower half of his face was covered with a thick foliage of white hair.

Karno nodded, and he was let in by the bearded man whom he had blackmailed less than twenty-four hours ago, who was also the writer of Karno's dreams. Talk about an embarrassing situation. Ananda Reza Chowdhury was wearing a grey Henley tee and a pair of grey pyjamas. His clothes lacked contrast, his presence as stoic as his invitation to his home on the phone the previous day.

Ananda pointed towards the couch and asked him to take a seat.

'Okay, so what's the catch?' Karno asked.

Ananda walked back to the kitchen, which was visible from the living room, started chopping onions and calmly said, 'What catch?'

Karno looked around the room to see if he could spot something which could be used as a weapon. Ananda Reza

Chowdhury looked like a harmless man, but he wanted to be prepared for the worst, just in case.

Usually if you're threatened by someone, especially a stranger, you would be inclined to feel hostility towards them. Karno expected that Ananda would call all his friends over to face this unknown visitor. There was also a small chance that he would call the cops on Karno. But all he had done was make a phone call from a public telephone. They couldn't really book him on any charges. And visiting someone's house isn't a crime.

But Chowdhury, like a seasoned novelist, had turned the tables.

'Sit down and tell me why you're here,' Chowdhury said. 'Suneeta won't be back before nine … You know Suneeta, surely?' he paused. Karno nodded politely. 'Thought so. She won't be back before nine; and I have a very tight schedule for the evening. I have to cook, finish edits on an article that I must submit by midnight, and listen to you. If you hurry up, I'd be rather grateful.'

It was evident to Karno that the power had shifted in their equation; Ananda was calling the shots now. He reminded himself that he hadn't matched with Reza Chowdhury on a dating app and this wasn't their first date. He tried to relax, took a seat on the couch, and began.

'My name is Karno …'

'Is that relevant to your story?' Chowdhury said, wiping his tears from cutting onions.

Karno couldn't find an adequate response to that question.

'Anyway, please continue,' he prompted.

'First, I want to apologize to you for the way I approached you.' He needed to get this thought off his chest, to let Ananda know that he wasn't really like the person he must have sounded like on the telephone.

But instead of looking relieved, Ananda seemed disappointed. 'That's anti-climactic,' he said.

The uneasiness and hesitation in Karno's movements were so palpable that it was hard to miss. He wasn't used to interacting with unknown faces, unless it was for books in Intezaar Sahab's bookshop. Recommending authors was what he was good at, not interrogating them. Countless times he had suggested a stranger pick up an Ananda Reza Chowdhury title from the store, but now that the man was in front of him, he fumbled to even speak a word without caution. He was finally beginning to believe that old saying: never meet your heroes.

Unlike his writing – that marched with precision; his sentences always so meticulously crafted and mellifluous that often they wouldn't just tell a story, they would sing – he was a bitter man.

'Do you want some coffee, young man?' he asked, breaking Karno's train of thought. 'Say yes, since I definitely need some. The way you're progressing, you'll put me to sleep in the next five minutes,' he laughed. Karno wasn't sure whether he was laughing at Karno or because he was delighted with his own sense of humour. And he had already begun to address Karno as 'young man', as if he was some long-lost uncle with whom Karno was reuniting after years.

Ten minutes later, he came back from the kitchen and sat next to Karno. Two bone China cups, filled to the brim with black bitter coffee, were placed on the table in front of them. 'I would suggest gulp it down,' Ananda said with a grin. 'Or else you won't wake up.'

He was like a school bully brought out of Karno's past and placed in front of him in an old man's clothing.

'Now why don't you start again? Without beating around the bush this time,' he said.

Sex – usually the word people use to get someone's attention. Whether it's a campus corridor or a corporate conference room, it's that magical arrangement of letters which works everywhere. What you do with that attention is entirely up to you. Karno knew that wouldn't work here. What word or phrase could be more memorable and ostentatious than that?

What would make this outrightly obnoxious man patiently give his ear to Karno? A word he could utter that would restore the power balance in his favour.

Devaki.

Yes, Devaki.

That's the word he was searching for.

'Devaki,' he said.

Ananda sat still and didn't look at Karno, but his face betrayed the sudden shift in his feelings. The look on his face, which for so long was of a man who was pleased to be winning a trifle game of one-upmanship, had turned sombre.

'I'm here for her,' Karno went on. Seeing his opponent lose a point gracefully, some amount of assurance in his voice had also returned. Now he was ready to share her story … their story.

Ananda remained silent. Noticing an opportunity to take matters further into his own hands, Karno said, 'I know you want me out of your hair quickly. Believe me, I want the same thing. If you stop moving around the house like a child and stop wasting time making snide remarks for just a few minutes, we can get this over with quickly.'

After taking a sip of the coffee, Karno started narrating. He didn't miss a beat, didn't misquote a line; his narration didn't overlook any of the significant moments which Devaki and he had shared, or the details of his subsequent discovery of her reality.

For nearly twenty minutes, he held the rapt attention of a seasoned novelist – not disclosing important information all at once, but only as per the demand of the story. Ananda's mood, predictably, switched from disbelief to amazement to utterly overwhelmed by the time Karno said, 'That's the end.'

Stillness settled inside the room once Karno was done talking.

Yes, it was all a bit too much to swallow; even though once taken apart, none of the pieces of that story was too shocking for the times they were living through. That Devaki was odd and could well be a bit batty, Karno had understood, even though he hadn't met the real one. People sought a remedy for their loneliness wherever they found an opening, a crack in the door. That's where a place like FIND A FRIEND had come in and put a literal price tag on every life, whether dead or alive. Aren't we sometimes frightened of the very things we are thankful for? The world has for long been busy getting disintegrated with an unusual immediacy, prompting people to find solace, however unreal, in a short-lived but authentic experience, as a compulsion, like food and shelter; a secret desire which necessitated priority.

Ananda understood that.

And yet there was disbelief. Like there is when you're entering a beach town by road, and you start hearing the waves crashing on the shore before you can even see it.

17

When you put two writers together in a room, a lot is desired from them. If you're watching them through a CCTV camera, you would expect them to make things interesting, strike up an engaging conversation, add a dramatic flair to anything that they say. Going from 'I have come all the way just for you,' to 'And now that I have found you, you must die,' in a heartbeat. Like a matador and a bull, opponents bound together who complement each other as they enthral the crowd.

But that's rarely the case. They are usually left either searching for the right words or displaying a visible bitterness about each other's accomplishments. Unless they're both equally unsuccessful, in which case there's a good chance for a new friendship to bloom.

Ananda and Karno both knew from the moment they met that they could never be friends. But they had two very significant things in common: Devaki and the writing life. And by 'writing life', one doesn't mean J.K. Rowling's life or Kurt Vonnegut's life or Arundhati Roy's life, which is no less than a fight. Not the famous writer's writing life, but simply a writer's life. One that is made up of the struggles and sacrifices one must make to sustain the writing; which seldom presents an easy way out; which often just means living in self-doubt and disappointment; which poses more queries than it gives answers: Why do this at all?

That life in which writing isn't an alternative but a compulsion. Not a romantic notion but a synonym of the chemical element O in the periodic table.

They were those people. People who don't always become household names, but remain important, because writers are essential – for their empathy and ingenuity, and for noticing things in real life which others often miss. Once someone had asked Karno this question: Why write at all? He had shrugged and said, 'You gotta do what you gotta do.' He was thankful to the person for not asking in return what he meant by that. He'd just said something he had heard a character say in a film. Possibly an assassin who was asked the same question.

A writer and a hired assassin have a lot in common too. Both risk their lives each time they pick up their weapon of choice to sit and aim at something far, something faint and distant, expecting to hit the mark when nobody is watching.

'We don't have a narrator,' Ananda said. They had been sitting without saying a word for some time until Ananda finally breached the silence. Some people just talk in deceptive semantics. Pessimists and poets, especially. If they learnt that the world was about to end in a few hours, they wouldn't come and tell you that. Instead, they would say make a list of all the things you have always wanted to do but haven't yet, then burn it.

'What do we require a narrator for?' Karno had to ask. Some statements are auto-tuned that way. They don't appear alone but always paired with a question that follows them.

Ananda had lit a hand-rolled cigarette and was holding it between the fingers of his left hand. He resembled some kind of a modern, middle-aged Bengali detective. He sat with his legs crossed and stared at the print of an Édouard Vuillard painting on the wall, as if the faceless woman kissing a bearded man in the painting was withholding all the answers which could solve the mystery that was Devaki. Karno would later learn that it has been widely speculated that the woman in the painting was none other than Vuillard's own sister. And the bearded man in it was Vuillard himself. It's known both as *The Kiss* and *Self-Portrait with Sister*.

'No one is telling us our story,' he spoke again after a fleeting interval. 'We are living it in real time; you know that, right? Where we go from here isn't up to some divine plan – no matter what jagratas every winter and our news channels every evening try to tell you.'

Then he paused to check if Karno was listening to him. Even he knew he could be too much. 'You need to tell me what you want from me. Why are you here?'

'For your help,' Karno said.

'You would have to be more specific, Karno. It's been so many years, over a decade, since I last met her. Or even saw her. Besides, who you knew isn't really her. Just some odd, imagined version of her. How can I be of any help to you?'

Asking the obvious thing, that which has been lingering in the back of your mind, can be the trickiest thing to do. You can imagine a hundred questions in a thousand different ways, but there are only a handful of polite ways to ask them.

'Where is she?'

But that was not what Karno meant to say.

The things he wanted to ask were:

'What happened between the two of you?'

'Why did she go away?'

'Did you do something to her?'

'Do you know if something terrible happened to her?'

'Did you in any way harm her?' Or worse – 'Did you kill her?'

Ananda gave him a stupefied look and said, 'You think I know her whereabouts and choose to not bring it up even after hearing everything you have just told me?'

How was Karno to know what Ananda was thinking? What if he actually got rid of her after forcing her to cut a deal with those shady FIND A FRIEND people? It couldn't be for the money those guys offer; even though Ananda and Suneeta's 2 BHK apartment looked neat, it was hardly what one would call opulent. The living room where they were seated was surprisingly sparse with a couple of bookshelves and a small wooden table placed in the centre. It didn't have a couch which is a common feature in most Indian homes. Several neatly woven wicker chairs, painted the colour of earth, populated the room, but all at a two-arm's length from each other in the rather spread-out area. Lineage of a household that believes in social interactions but never unrestrained intimacy.

What if Ananda had a debt which he needed to repay? Maybe loan sharks were after his life, and the easiest remedy for him was to trade Devaki's life story. What if she had refused? Could that have been a reason why he felt it was necessary to get her out of the way?

But even in his head it all seemed a tad improbable. A simple online search could show that although companies like FAF were growing in number and slowly becoming commonplace, they were still more the exception than the norm. People, for some inexplicable reason, still liked other people more. Even if they had sufficient financial backing and potential for a sustainable future, it was still unlikely that they'd become another Apple or Microsoft in the foreseeable future. Therefore, in case Ananda had a role to play in Devaki's disappearance, the motive couldn't have been financial. Because even though Karno found Ananda to be untrustworthy, it was also true that Devaki had herself dealt with the strange man who went by the name of Mr Brown at FAF.

If at all Ananda was involved, the reason had to be personal. And in order to make him confess, Karno had to catch him off guard – take the bails off when he lifted his foot even a millimetre from the ground.

'Was it you …?' Karno said.

Finish your sentences, for heaven's sake, Ananda's expression seemed to exclaim.

'Did you …?'

'Did I what?'

Strangely, Karno could detect a hint of a smile on Ananda's face. As if he knew what Karno was about to say next and was laughing at his hesitancy. More than his suspicion that one of his favourite writers could be a cold-blooded murderer, it was his own predictability that enraged him.

'Go on,' Ananda said.

'Are you responsible for her disappearance?'

Ananda didn't flinch, but his smile broadened. 'You mean to ask if I murdered her, stuffed her body in a gunny bag and then threw it in a river somewhere?'

That description was very specific, almost a little too specific, Karno thought. And Ananda said it with such conviction that it almost sounded true. Like when you set your watch five minutes ahead to have those few extra minutes every day – to sleep, to get to work, to catch a train, to make a decision – yet each time you look at it you realize it's a deceit; but you also know that while it's not true, it's still near truth. Even if one hand of the watch is lying, the other is in all possibility telling the truth.

'No,' he continued. 'She isn't floating underneath any water body anywhere. In fact …' he paused for effect and looked Karno in the eye. 'In fact, she is in the other room.'

A startled Karno looked around immediately, just one note less than frantically. Had she been here all this while, all these years, he thought. It was all he wanted; to ensure that she was safe and doing all right. To see her once, so he could tell her all about how he fell in love with her, that a part of him will always be. He wanted to know how she looked; did she have silver hair now?

Ananda recognized Karno's restlessness and asked, 'Do you want to go to our study and say hello to her?'

Was that really a possibility? Would he find her if he just walked into the next room? But Ananda lived with Suneeta, his partner of some years, he thought. Was he suggesting that all three of them lived together in the same house … partners and ex-lovers under the same roof? He wondered if Devaki and Suneeta got along.

'I know you want to, Karno,' he continued. 'But I am afraid you can't do that.'

'Why not?'

'Oh, because she is buried in the wall. And we got the house painted last month, or else I would have let you break it down.' Karno felt squeamish just imagining it. 'Plus, the smell,' he continued. 'It is revolting how corpses smell, especially these ancient ones. Takes nearly a week of cleansing and sanitizing to drive it away.'

Karno shook his head in disapproval when he understood what Ananda was doing. 'Do you really think it is okay to joke about such things?'

'What?' he replied. 'You didn't like it? It's a small tribute to my favourite Hindi film – *Mughal-e-Azam*.'

How was he to communicate with this man who seemed to have shut all doors on himself before Karno could even knock on them. Strange that he had found it much simpler to connect with Devaki, who was essentially an electronic device, not very different from a television set or an Alexa, in the shape of a human being – so much so that it had brought him to Ananda's doorstep. And here he was, unable to negotiate with someone who was just like him – made of flesh, blood and real feelings, allegedly.

18

SUNEETA AND ANANDA HAd met a few months after he had separated from his ex-wife and a couple of years since she had been involved with someone seriously. It wasn't in New Delhi, where they had lived separately at one point and lived together now. It was on a book tour, one of the very last ones he ever did. He hated the whole enterprise from the core of his heart: going around bookstores and venues across the country and reading from his work, answering inane questions from strangers, like 'Is this book autobiographical?' And then inevitably coming back from it after having offended someone with his answers; 'It's a memoir titled *Vignettes of My Ordinary Life*, how did you come up with this absolutely groundbreaking thought?'

Calcutta, the city of Ananda's birth, was where they first met. He was seeing a few friends at the Indian Coffee House in College Street, *just like old times*, as one of his Presidency classmates had said to him over the phone. She had just finished a performance at the Academy of Fine Arts and landed up at the Coffee House with some local members of her troupe.

They were seated at adjacent tables, and he was discussing with his friends how writing a memoir could be the most liberating experience for a writer. 'Because what better subject is there in this world but oneself. It's a meditative, immersive process of research like any other – only the library where you pull up a chair and sit down every morning is your own heart. And the act of entering and leaving those premises is a journey inward.'

She overheard, like most people in such settings do, and said, 'But that's a privilege not everyone gets to enjoy, isn't it? It might be a process that's worked for you, but you certainly cannot generalize.' All this without an introduction or a hello; regulars of the establishment would vouch that this happened routinely on its hallowed ground. Ananda, who used to spend several hours there every afternoon during the days of his youth, knew that even if everything outside its gates changed, even if Calcutta became another Shanghai, as ministers and industrialists keep promising, certain Coffee House rituals were meant to last forever.

It was presumed by everyone present at the scene – those who knew Ananda's self-absorbed nature and those who didn't know him but were still aware of it, because for some men their reputation always precedes them – that Ananda would feel challenged. Some were excited by the potential of a charged up room, for who wouldn't want to sit with a hot cup of coffee and dunkable rusks in hand and watch two bright minds take on each other like two wrestlers in a steel cage match. Some also feared that Ananda and his ego would drown either in combat or in self-loathing, ensuring that the audience too sinks with him.

But everybody was proven wrong that day.

Suneeta did not make him feel attacked or confronted. Instead, what she left him feeling was a form of ebullience – and a sense of thrill and excitement took over him for which there was no definite explanation. Like being stuck at a boring party with a group of insurance agents and suddenly watching someone new walk in, maybe a ballerina or a Phoebe Waller-Bridge lookalike, someone very likely to turn the night around. In Ananda's mind, his otherwise mundane existence was unexpectedly imbued with possibilities. Men overthink; men who write, criminally so. He felt younger.

19

THERE WAS NO MURDER. As it turned out, nothing out of the ordinary had happened between Ananda and Devaki. Except for the self-conscious equation which they shared and tried hiding from the world, there was nothing else to it. It was like any other affair between any two people. Karno came back from Ananda's house with no answers but also with a fresh dose of optimism. Crimes of passion, it seems, are more common in mystery novels than in reality. Real life is crueller than that. Here, when people get bitter, instead of murder, they just choose to forget about all the good things the other person did for them and learn to carry on without them; like nothing has happened. And even if something shifts inside them, like when a powerful earthquake splits a tectonic plate into two and pushes them apart, even then they teach themselves to disguise it well.

The last thing Ananda said to him that day was, 'Come back when you're less angry, and I'll tell you about the last time we spoke. When we are driven by rage, we find it hard to listen to others, usually because everything is too loud inside of us.'

So that's where he was. Back from his tiny expedition. And also, back to his old friends again. Rhea and Sandip. They hadn't separated or anything; they just saw less of each other once Devaki came into Karno's life. A temporary hiatus. But not in a negative way. There just isn't enough time in a day when you're trying to get to know one person intimately for you to be able to see your friends too.

It is not that they never complained about his prolonged absences from their lives. And whenever they did, Karno would remain quiet and hear them out patiently, until they had let out all their frustrations and eventually started feeling bad for him. Then they had to hug it out. It was an old but dependable method, which Karno found rather useful. He knew they knew he was manipulating them in some weird way, and that made it easier for his conscience to deal with the situation.

When they heard about Devaki, one of them just said, 'Oh.' And the other thought for a second before observing, 'I really thought you had finally found a decent one, but at the same time wondered how. Now it all makes sense.' That's it. Not a word more. Was it really that simple? To accept uncomfortable truths and carry on? Then why couldn't he? Were Rhea and Sandip not right in the head, or was he the odd one out? Was he stuck in the wrong friendship? Or worse, should he have been born many years ago and was stuck in the wrong time? But at the same time, he reminded himself that isolated people need not necessarily be the prisoners to their own sadness.

Rhea recommended that he should definitely get on a dating app without wasting any more time. They both agreed he should start dating someone new and that could considerably reduce the span of this whole forgetting-and-moving-on phase. Karno told them that he had tried; he reminded them about Suchitra. 'What happened there?' Sandip asked. 'Didn't you have a good time with her?' He did. She was all kinds of wonderful. But that was not the point. He was seeking a particular kind of intimacy that he couldn't explain. That perfect mix of attention and indifference, which he had experienced with her – Devaki, not Suchitra. Not anybody else, before or after.

However, all that had to wait, love or its likeness that Karno hoped to find. That evening when he returned home after seeing his friends, Karno received a call from his father. When the phone rang, he stared at the screen for so long that it eventually stopped ringing, and he had to call him back.

He hadn't received a call from his father's number in years. When his mother called him and his father happened to be around, he sometimes took the cell from her to say hello to him and ask if he needed anything. But the ten-digit number saved as 'Dad' on Karno's phone had had no use over the last many years. It was possible that his father felt the same way too, because Karno never made an effort to reach out to him either; barring the customary phone call on Bijoya Dashami, which had become some sort of a ritual between them; they only talked when Karno visited his parents in Calcutta. That was why he couldn't process seeing his father's name, blinking on his phone screen, for the first few seconds.

His father picked up, and before Karno could say anything, he said, 'Come home.' Then he began talking to someone else in a voice that reflected urgency and trepidation. That's all he conveyed to Karno, an instruction to return without a beginning or an end. Just the crucial, bare-bones centre, like a declaration made by a character during the interval of a film, right before dying or leaving permanently.

He waited, holding the phone close to his ear, for about a minute, trying to overhear every sound, every breath which reached the receiver from the other end and picked up singular words like 'drunk', 'hurt', 'crash', 'ambulance'. Fragments which didn't have much meaning of their own, but when put together, guessing what he had to prepare himself for in a matter of mere seconds became easier.

His father returned to him after finishing his conversation with whoever he was speaking with. 'Your mother was in a car crash, Karno. Just come home as soon as you can, please.'

Karno got a bad taste in his mouth, like the air he was breathing was a mixture of oxygen and aluminium, how he felt when his mother made him swallow a bitter medicine as a child. Then he said, 'Is she … going to be okay?'

Asim, Karno's headstrong father, who always preferred to have the last word, remained silent.

His mother didn't drive. She was so terrified of the thought that if she was driving, then her or someone else's life would be in her hands. It was easier for her to trust Karno, or his father, or even a stranger, than herself when it came to driving a car. Then who was driving the car she was in when it crashed? What did it crash against? Another car? Are those people all right? He wasn't trying to be kind or selfless. But by thinking about others who may have been present with his mother during the frightening accident, he was able to shift his thoughts from the image of his mother lying on a hospital bed, surrounded by electronic devices emitting red and green lights, like a fortune teller machine, struggling to keep her body alive.

'Dad …?' Karno mumbled.

This time he replied, 'They're trying. She is under observation in the ICU. Take the next flight to Calcutta. Do you have money?'

'Which hospital?'

'Woodlands … come soon,' came the reply.

20

EVERYTHING WAS IN A haze, until Karno saw his mother's tired face. The flight; the cab ride to the hospital; the phone call to his father informing him that his flight had landed; and the colours of the city that grew up with him and around him for the first twenty-odd years of his life, passing by outside the cab window.

His father touched his shoulder with a gentleness he couldn't remember him ever showing before. Raja da, who worked in a clerical position at his father's office and also Asim's man Friday, appeared out of nowhere and held Karno's hand, guiding him through the narrow alleyways of the hospital building, towards the Intensive Care Unit where his mother was resting.

He could see her face through a tiny glass window. She looked like she was fast asleep. But that's also how people looked when they had passed away in their bed. Karno had noticed it when his grandmother had died and her body was kept in their house for a few hours for close friends and relatives to pay her a last visit. Although he couldn't understand what difference it would have made to her, the one who was already gone. He was only fourteen then. It was much later that he realized death isn't ever about the one who passes away but about those they leave behind.

A doctor arrived and informed Karno that he could go and see his mother. He knew that lady was a doctor because she was wearing a white coat. It's easy to trust someone in a white coat at a hospital, unlike, say, at a casino. She could have just as easily been a woman who thought it was time for Karno to see his mother, someone who was coincidentally wearing a white coat.

He could see that his mother was asleep or in a limbo, one of the two things, but not awake. She had a white bandage wrapped around her skull. In fact, he found it a little too white upon looking closely, like Surf Excel-advertisement white, as if some assistant had wrapped it around her head only for this one scene and an invisible director was waiting to call 'cut' once it was over, and then his mother would sit up and ask for a cup of Darjeeling tea. Like she was some celebrity actor working in a commercial for an exorbitant fee. Which made Karno pause in his imagination for she was always uncomfortable even while posing for a family photograph. Karno closed his eyes for a moment and pictured the dry blood on the other side of the bandage.

Nobody had told him yet how she had got there. Where was she headed when her journey was abruptly cut short? If she never woke up again, Karno thought, he would want to know where she was going that day, what were her final thoughts. He shook his head. He was getting ahead of himself. She was still breathing; still the one who had birthed and raised him, not some mass of nothingness.

He didn't want to go any closer to his mother. They didn't speak much any more, not since he moved out of their home and went to New Delhi. He remembered how she always had trouble sleeping. It looked like she was finally able to take a peaceful nap, and he didn't want to disturb that.

Asim came and stood next to him. He asked him if his flight was okay. What if there really was some glitch with his flight, how did it matter now? Would his father go back in time and fix things? And if he indeed could, shouldn't he have better things to fix then? In his life, in his wife Mala's life, and in his only son Karno's life? But Karno didn't say any of these things; he knew how his father's priorities had always been a little skewed. He nodded and said the flight was fine.

'How did this happen?' he asked Asim.

He took a moment, then said, 'We were on our way to the cinema. Priya is doing some special screenings of old Bengali and English classics, and your mother really wanted to watch *Apur Sansar* again, but on the big screen, since she couldn't when it was originally released. You know how much I hate going to the theatre, but this time I—'

'You were in the car with her?' Karno didn't let his father finish.

'Yes,' Asim said.

In that moment, he was disturbed by the fact that while his mother was fighting for her life in the ICU, his father looked completely fine with not even a scratch on his body. Despite being in the same car as her at the time of the accident.

'Are you okay?' he asked.

'I am absolutely fine,' Asim replied.

'Were you driving?'

Asim met his son's gaze and said, 'You know I always drive my own car and detest being driven around by someone else.' Karno didn't say anything else, but he didn't look away either, to ensure that his father could hear his silence and feel the quiet accusing rage which was festering inside him.

Luckily, Raja da could read the situation and suggested that he and Karno grab coffee from the hospital canteen, since Karno had made up his mind about not seeing his mother again in that state. They sat down close enough for them to be able to hear each other, maintaining just that wee bit of distance that employees and sons of their employers always keep between them.

'What's going on here, Raja da? At least you must tell me,' Karno did not wait too long before asking him.

Raja realized he couldn't postpone this cumbersome conversation, and the sooner it got over the easier he would feel around Karno. 'Like your father said, Karno. He was driving, your mother was in the passenger seat next to him. They were on the E.M. Bypass near the Science City, a bus tried to overtake his car from the wrong side and hit your father's car—'

Karno interrupted him to ask, 'And he didn't notice?'

'You know, Karno, your father has poor vision in his left eye. Besides, the bus was moving at a very high speed …'

'Does he not realize that every time he is driving a vehicle, he isn't just putting his own life at risk but several others …'

'You know very well, Karno, that your father doesn't trust anyone else when it comes to driving. He doesn't feel safe.'

'Well, isn't that ironic,' Karno said.

Raja wanted to nod in agreement but, being a loyal employee of Karno's father, he didn't. He kept his palm gently on Karno's arm, which was resting on the table between them, and said, 'Have faith, please.'

'What about the airbag?' Karno asked.

With slight hesitation in his voice, Raja said, 'Oh … they were travelling in your father's old car which doesn't have those. His new car is automatic, and he still feels uncomfortable driving it around.'

An unmistakable expression of irritation flitted across Karno's face. 'Then why did he even buy the new car?'

'For you. That's what he said.'

'Are you fucking kidding me?' Karno blurted out, unable to hold back his exasperation any longer.

'Relax, Karno,' Raja said. 'Your mother will get better ...' Then he paused before repeating, '... Have faith.'

'It's like you rehearsed your lines before coming here to talk to me,' Karno told him.

This kind of loss is the hardest. When you are acutely aware that you are about to lose someone or something important – a mother, a home, a city – and that you did not play any role in reaching that point. When it was just handed to you – this crucial moment in life that will shape your entire existence; and yet you were never in control of how you got there. The more Raja assured him that his mother was going to be okay, the more certain he was that she would not make it out of that Intensive Care Unit alive. It is just how some people's minds work; they are so not used to hope that positivity makes them more pessimistic.

When Devaki left, Karno was left with a giant hole in his heart, the size of a crater on the moon. When his mother leaves, whether it is that day or a few days or a few months or even some years later, he would be left with another, even larger crater-sized hole in his heart. Will his father too feel the same way?

'Will Dad be left with a giant hole in his heart, Raja da?' he said.

'Sorry? What?'

'If Ma dies, will Dad too have a huge, unfillable hollowness grow inside him?'

'I don't understand,' Raja said confusedly. 'What are you asking?'

Karno's eyes were fixed on the pendulum of the clock that was on the wall behind Raja. He didn't speak at first. When Raja asked again, he muttered, 'Nothing,' and got up to leave.

As he turned around, his eyes fell on a colourful poster that was hanging near the exit door, which he hadn't noticed while walking in. It had the image of a snow-clad mountain and the sun rising from behind its peak. At the bottom of the image, in bold, black letters it was written: 'Have faith'.

21

THREE DAYS LATER, KARNO'S fifty-something mother, started feeling a little bit better. She came to her senses and asked for water. Then she said she was hungry and asked if she could eat pizza, a request which the doctor had to refuse. A couple more days passed in the hospital, and then she was discharged. There were several minor injuries on her body and one of her knees might be permanently damaged, but she was doing well otherwise. The doctor warned them that because of the immense shock of the accident, some of her memories could become muddled, which could occasionally make her confused. But he also gave them the assurance that in all probability she would slowly start going back to leading a normal life again.

It was about a month later that they realized the diagnosis wasn't going to come true. Karno sat by his mother's side all through that difficult month, often not saying anything, just staying next to her holding her hand. Sometimes he'd pick up a book from her shelf and start reading from a page opened at random. He couldn't tell if she was listening; when her eyes would moisten, he liked to believe it was because she was paying attention to his reading. But he also thought it could be from a memory fading in front of her mind's eyes, an old scene from her life dissolving bit by bit.

There were blood clots in her brain that grew increasingly resilient as each day passed. Asim and Karno avoided each other in the house as much as they could. Except exchanging the occasional nods and hellos when they crossed each other on the stairs or when they happened to be in the kitchen together searching for a midnight snack. Less like father and son, and more like prison inmates who share adjacent cells and see each other every day during their designated time out in the sun.

A nurse took care of Mala's needs twenty-four seven. Karno knew she was gradually coasting away from them. She was seldom there even when she was awake, staring at the ceiling for hours like she could see the sky beyond the concrete roof. Every now and then, she would scream in immense physical pain, without letting any words out, as if she had forgotten her entire vocabulary. Only her groans could be heard from the other room, where Karno would sit with his palms tightly shutting his ears. The nurse would give her painkillers, she'd drift in and out of consciousness, their numbered days together – mother, father, nurse and son – would pass that way.

Karno heard his father tell his uncle, Mala's brother, on the phone, 'Come see her one last time.' Which he did. He wasn't always around or seen much, like most other relatives who existed in the periphery of their social life, dropping in on an odd Christmas eve or for a dinner with cousins, which happened once every year.

While overhearing that phone conversation, Karno realized that his father believed she wasn't going to be around whenever that dinner happened next. That thought hurt him even more than seeing his mother writhing in pain. It is widely believed that there are five stages of grief: denial, anger, bargaining, depression and acceptance. But if this sequence is disturbed, if acceptance comes even before denial for someone else, it becomes a hard pill to swallow for the rest whose feelings are following the order.

While leaving, his uncle gave Karno a hug and said, 'She's not going to make it. I hope you're preparing yourself for that?'

Karno meant to say, 'You're no medical expert, you don't know shit, you better keep your trap shut.' But as always, he didn't say what he actually felt and decided to make do with a nod instead. The man, however, was unwilling to give up until he had elicited an actual response from his nephew, one constructed of words and not gestures.

'You should start getting ready for a life without your mother. We are all going to lose a huge part of ourselves with her gone – your father, you, I, and several other people whose lives she touched.'

'Well, you're right about that last bit,' Karno responded this time. 'But I'm not someone who considers a person gone while they're still here.'

As soon as he finished speaking, he turned around to go inside his mother's room and shut the door gently … so it wouldn't wake her up.

While on his way out of her room one day, he heard her call out his name. It was late, well past midnight, and she should have been asleep by then. Although it had become increasingly harder to tell when she was sleeping and when she wasn't. 'Karno,' she said a second time, which was when he was sure he had heard it right.

'You remember my name?' He sat down on the chair next to her bed.

'Of course,' she replied. 'But why do you look so different?'

Karno touched his face to check if he could feel any change. 'Do I?' he said.

'Yes,' his mother said. 'You're seven years old, but you look like a grown man. That's not how you were yesterday.'

He entwined his fingers in hers and said, 'Where are you, Ma?'

She did not say anything.

'Are you in the past now, Ma?' Karno asked again.

Again she remained silent, and this time for much longer. Her pulse had become so faint that even though she was breathing, almost all signs of life seemed to have left her body. Several minutes passed without either of them saying another word. Her eyes were closed, so Karno thought she must have nodded off. He delicately untangled their fingers and got up to leave. When he was at the door, he heard that pale, dimming voice once again.

'You might be done with the past, Karno. But is the past done with you yet?'

One night Karno came home drunk and headed straight for his father's room. Drunk would be understating it, for he could hardly balance himself on his two feet. He was hammered from head to toe. He meant to go to his room, hoping to pass out and forget about everything for the night. But habit is an unfaithful ally. This was his childhood home, after all. Even though he had left years ago, his muscles remembered the floor of this house like a pianist remembers the keys of a grand piano.

Seated on a wooden easy chair, Asim was reading a book that he promptly put down when he saw his son enter the room. The chair was always placed near the eastern wall of his room, next to a window, so that Asim could have his morning tea and read the newspaper while welcoming the day's first ray of sunlight. This was a scene Karno had seen repeat in front of him ever since he was a child. The chair used to be different – an older model that Asim had inherited from his father – but the setting remained unchanged. And perhaps so was Asim.

He watched Karno stumble, then manage himself sloppily as he walked inside. Something altered in his face and his gait immediately after he saw Asim. If you have ever walked into the wrong room by mistake while staying in a hotel, then you'll be able to imagine what he looked like. Asim could spot his discomfort almost instantly, as Karno stared at the red oxide floor – a traditional marker of old Calcutta homes, now on the verge of disappearing from the face of the city.

Searching for something perfunctory to say before leaving, Karno asked, 'What are you reading?' without looking at Asim.

Asim took off his glasses and asked Karno to sit down, pointing at the divan placed right next to the door. When his son didn't move, Asim's instruction changed into a request, 'Please,' he pleaded, 'sit down and talk to your father at least once.' Karno was not used to declining his father, so he did as he was told.

'Happy now?' Karno said as he sat down. 'Now tell me, what's that book you're reading?'

'What are you doing?' Asim said without answering him once again. 'I have never seen you spiralling out of control in front of me before.'

Karno didn't wait for even a second before answering him. He said, 'I have also never seen you try to kill my mother before now.'

If Asim was shocked, he didn't let it show. Men hide their feelings all their life and eventually make a mistake that can't be undone.

'Ask what you want to ask me,' Asim said. 'But do it while looking into my eyes, with your spine straight and no hesitation in your voice. Not like some miserable, sympathy-seeking fool whose senses have ceased to function, because he is too busy feeling sorry for himself.'

That distinguishable timbre of his voice was back, which Karno could identify even among a thousand chiming voices. 'What happened to Ma?' Karno muttered, his words barely audible.

His father took a deep breath and replied as calmly as he could, 'You already know what happened, baba. We were in an accident.' Karno had expected this answer, but hearing the word 'baba' threw him off a bit. What was it but affection; this unbridled, unexpected show of love. 'I wasn't prepared for this,' he wanted to tell his father. As if he was appearing for some exam and had encountered a question from a section which wasn't in the syllabus.

There was one thing Karno had meant to ask ever since he got there but had not been able to gather the courage for. This was the most convenient opportunity he would get, he thought, and said, 'How come you're not hurt then? How come only she has major injuries, only she's suffering, and you're all right?'

The truth was that it was sheer luck. Asim didn't have any answer for Karno – who passed out on the divan in his father's room just a few seconds after asking the question. For a long time he would go on blaming his father for his mother's fate. It would only be many years later that he would learn it was, in fact, his mother, who, crushed by a moment of unexpected sorrow, had veered the steering wheel of their car with her hands, and before Asim could regain control of the vehicle, it had gone and smashed into another car speeding from the opposite direction. Karno would spend all those years in the middle – between his mother's accident and finding out the truth about it – blaming Asim for her misfortune. They so rarely talked to one another that Mala had never mentioned to her son how she had been suffering for more than two years before the incident, how she was seeing a psychologist and was put on medication.

Ever since that day in Darjeeling when Mala and Asim decided to not part ways, their sole motivation had been to raise Karno in the right way, imparting their principles and moulding him in a way they thought was best for him. Asim and Mala had always wanted different things from life. The more they drifted apart with time, the farther they found Karno from themselves too. Then came a point when he had sailed far past the horizon and disappeared from their sight entirely. Once again, Asim, Mala and their marriage – gasping for air – were left alone to suffer together purposelessly.

No one knows why Asim couldn't tell Karno the truth. Perhaps he thought it's better that Karno hated one parent more than before, if it meant he would realize he loved the other one more than he had known. In Asim's silence, Karno finally discovered the words he had been searching for to say to his mother. The next morning, when Asim stood near the door to Mala's room he could hear Karno's voice. 'Don't go, Ma,' he said to his mother. And then they cried.

22

BACK IN NEW DELHI, Karno found himself at the doorstep of Ananda once again.

He had returned after spending three months in Calcutta, looking after his mother while forgetting to look after himself. It had begun to haunt him; that house, and the air inside it. So one day Karno called the doctor and asked if his mother would live, and once he was assured by the doctor that she wasn't going anywhere anytime soon, he had decided to leave his home without saying a word to his father.

Ananda opened the door and asked him to come in like he was expecting Karno. It was a Saturday, and Suneeta was home too. She was sitting at the dining table reading a copy of *The Caravan* magazine; its cover had a blown-up photograph of a big Bollywood star whose Indian citizenship was often questioned by the media, so he had been trying to establish his patriotism through his films for the past few years.

Karno instantly took a liking to her. Anybody who read the kind of books and magazines he liked to read couldn't be too different from him, he thought. A dangerous hypothesis to live by, but in this case it worked.

Suneeta smiled a big, knowing smile when Ananda introduced Karno, who was confused by her reaction. There was no real reason for her to have been so glad to see Karno, but perhaps that was just how she lived her life.

Perhaps people like Suneeta, and to some extent even Ananda, knew how to embrace something which didn't belong to them – to make the unfamiliar a part of their inner world when they desired. Or maybe it was all an act; she worked in theatre, after all.

'You look terrible,' was the first thing Suneeta said to Karno.

He knew she was right. Karno hadn't bathed after getting back from Calcutta the previous evening, and he hadn't changed either. Still smelling like airports and resembling a train wreck, here he was in full glory. Standing in front of two people he barely knew, hoping they would help him find answers to the questions he hadn't been able to frame yet.

'Come, sit down,' she said. 'Do you want a cup of tea? I am having some. It is a bright Saturday morning, have some tea with me, then go ahead and talk to Ananda about whatever you have come here for.' Karno liked her presence yet wanted to distrust her intentions. But the truth was that he had met other people like her before. Those who received the world without any scepticism.

Intezaar Sahab who had welcomed Karno into his bookstore and made him a small part of it was one such person. So was his mother, when she was much younger and whenever she was not around her husband. Everybody took to her unfeigned charm almost immediately after meeting her. Especially children, except Karno. And while she had loved him earnestly, every time she looked at Karno's face, it reminded her of her life which was collapsing before her own eyes. And she wasn't big-hearted enough to forgive him for that.

And Devaki. The one who came from the wild and became his home.

Karno pulled up a chair and sat down next to Suneeta.

When Karno was saying goodbye to his mother, she was feeling a lot better than before; she was able to talk, lift her head and look at her son's face whenever he was around. Karno had thought that she would try to stop him, ask him to stay. Since the accident, she had had several visitors but only her son to comfort her with prolonged moments of silence. More than any medicine, that is what helped her get through each day. But like children have a way of surprising their parents, parents too have their own ways of breaking their moulds of predictability.

She found it difficult to talk. Yet, somehow she had gathered strength from some corner of her body and said, 'Karno, don't come back.'

At first, Karno thought he heard it wrong. She couldn't be saying that, undoing everything he had prepared for, making the script he had religiously rehearsed in his head completely pointless.

'Don't come back,' she said to her son. 'There's nothing for you here except anguish and neglect. That's what you've always got from the two of us, because your father and I were busy looking for something in each other which we never possessed to begin with.' She took a deep breath; Karno asked her to stop talking and close her eyes. But she knew she couldn't keep these words inside herself any longer.

For the first time in he couldn't recall how many years, Karno's mother held his face in her hands. 'We lied, Karno,' she said. 'We lied to one another, and we lied to you. We lied when you were born, and we told everyone that we were starting a family. It's true that we raised you and loved you too, but that wasn't enough to make a family out of the three people who shared this house. From the day I moved here until the day you were born, the two of us held on to this pretence, but once you arrived, those shackles fell.'

'You don't need to do this, Ma,' he said, fearing her body might disintegrate.

But Mala was once again that twenty-year-old girl who played cricket with boys, contested the elections in her college, and was a constant defender of her will. 'None of us are bad people, baba,' she continued. That dreaded, dear, devastating 'baba' was back again in Karno's life. He sighed.

'As people we are all decent, kind of all right. In fact, we are all totally alike. Just how three fingers of the exact same size and shape cannot belong to the same hand, we don't either. Our lives are done now; you need to stop looking for your peace among us and go look for it where you know there's a chance. It's not here, Karno. Your life is not here.'

After taking that quick trip to his mother's room inside his mind, Karno was back on the chair next to Suneeta. Is this what being alive in the twenty-first century was like? Being split, being alive in multiple places at once.

'Does she …' He looked at Ananda. '… know about …?'

Ananda looked at him and said without equivocation, 'About Devaki? Of course. How old do you think we are? Twenty?'

'Did you tell her …' Karno was panting now. His words lacked direction. Like a device with just one per cent battery remaining, which, with its dying breath, was trying its best to establish contact with someone.

Ananda looked confused, and said, 'Tell her what?'

'What I told you, about how I met her …'

'Yes, I did,' Ananda replied.

Karno turned towards Suneeta, who simply smiled and nodded.

He had had it by then. Not being able to make sense of the world was one thing; he could live with that. He never expected too much from himself anyway. That was, for him, one of the most comforting things about being whoever he was. To exist being free from the burden of one's own expectations. But this was life treating him like a lab rat; he increasingly felt like an experiment that was bound to fail, but one that's going to be conducted anyway for the sake of the records.

He felt a sudden urge to bang his fists on the table, to let loose this time. Go berserk and dismantle the living room of this couple, whose behaviour seemed odd to him, whose reactions baffled him.

'What the fuck is wrong with you people?' Karno ultimately said without acting on any of his impulses. Only he said it much louder than he usually spoke. 'Don't you find any of this bizarre or strange at all? I met a woman who is literally a robot. A moving, talking machine that looks and speaks and makes love like the person you knew so many years ago.'

'So what?' Suneeta said this time. 'The world has long gone beyond calculators and computers ... if you don't wish to keep track, that is all right. We don't always either. But if you choose to not keep up, you will fall behind. That is the rule of the jungle. You eat or you get eaten. Or the third option, the safest bet for people like us ... you run. So no, it doesn't surprise us that you met an android version of my partner's ex-lover. Which was problematic in its own way, but that is for another day.'

She heaved a sigh of relief after this brief stint of opening up, and then said, 'This isn't the earth where we were born, Karno. Tomorrow you might hear that a baby has been born on Mars after human beings set up a colony there, or that an octopus is using its tentacles to fly a plane, who knows. Everything that we once thought impossible, we're living right at the centre of it now. Our planet is on its way to self-combust, and that's because we lost control a long time ago.'

'I don't understand …' Karno put his face on his knees and tried to shut the world out with his bare hands.

Suneeta touched his arm. 'And you don't need to. It isn't necessary to understand everything that you experience. Just protect your feelings, that is the only way you will survive.'

They were headed to the famous 4S bar in Defence Colony, a popular meeting point for many writers, journalists and lawyers for several years. Ananda insisted that Karno tag along. When Suneeta noticed Karno's hesitation, in a kind and soft voice she said to him, 'Come, if you aren't too busy. Sometimes you don't find answers to your questions where you're seeking them. So why not look everywhere?'

Karno didn't have any reason to say yes to that offer … so he did.

At the bar, a muted TV set was on where a young man, dressed as a geriatric and pretending to be older, was trying to sell electronic pets to his viewers. 'If you are ageing and alone, abandoned by your children, or recently widowed and unsure of how to fill a gaping void in your life – bring home a pet dog or a cat or a bunny rabbit (even an anteater) which runs on batteries and lets you pet them uninterrupted. The best part? You don't have to feed them or take them for walks. All you need to do is plug it in before going to bed at night, like a portable speaker or an electric shaver. You'll find it fully charged in the morning, waiting to serve you with its undivided attention and company once more.' Every sentiment had now conveniently become a button-operated utility.

Karno said hello to a few of their friends, then sat down with a bottle of beer without paying attention to what people around him were talking about. By the time his mind returned to the Earth after circling the rings of Saturn, a heated discussion had already begun. He would have rather gone home but couldn't think of a convincing excuse and had no choice but to survive the hellfire.

It didn't take him too long to realize that Ananda, without wasting a minute, had already told the group how Karno had met and fallen for a humanoid robot recently, and now they were each sharing their thoughts about it. Thankfully, he hadn't divulged any other details. Karno already hated the feeling that his private life was being dissected by total strangers in a dingy South Delhi watering hole. But now he didn't want to leave because he was also deriving some sort of perverse joy from it. His love life may have been a failure, but as an evening debate over cheap alcohol and stale fried snacks, it had the potential to become an astounding success.

'Do you even realize how big a political threat such a technology could become in the near future? For all of us?' The man sitting opposite Suneeta banged the table with a controlled movement of his arm to prove that he was making a crucial point. It was evident to all those who were present that he was hearing about the existence of such a technology for the first time.

'Everyone here agrees with you,' Suneeta responded calmly, 'you needn't get excited, Amol.'

'Why are you talking like someone who has discovered something hitherto unknown to humankind?' Ananda interjected with a hint of snarkiness in his tone.

Everyone looked at him, expecting him to dive straight into a dramatic monologue, because that is what public intellectuals are primarily known for. He adjusted himself in his seat as he tried to understand his assignment.

The man named Amol fixed his glasses, scratched his chin while in deep thought and then spoke again. 'I'm both amazed and appalled, Ananda, that a thinking individual like you isn't bothered by such a dangerous development that's happened in the name of innovation.'

Ananda smirked and said, 'I'm offended at how unaware you sound right now.'

Suneeta looked at him disapprovingly, a discreet look, shared only by couples, through which a person asks their partner to stop being condescending.

A woman sitting next to him said, 'Maybe you should start reading the news again,' and laughed. 'You seem to be stuck in the 1990s.'

'Do you know what's going on in the deepest, darkest corners of the forests of Chhattisgarh? How people survive there? The lengths they have to go to, to ensure their children don't go hungry. How they dodge a government bullet every single day by living a life in hiding? No, you don't. I do. So, my dear Ananda, I may be unaware of a lot of things which you people seem to have accepted gleefully, but we all belong to the world we have chosen to be a part of.'

The truth was the world had changed and continued changing far too quickly for the common citizen to match steps with it. Keeping up wasn't a matter of choice any longer. You either accepted and celebrated what was spoon-fed to you at jet speed or became irrelevant and outdated. Why one needed to upgrade their phones annually or throw away their old computers every three years for a new one wasn't a question anybody was supposed to ask any more. From a lifestyle choice it had turned into a survival strategy for most people. The day someone like Steve Jobs stepped on the big tech stage and proclaimed customers don't know what they want until you show it to them, the world changed forever.

'We've been living with many things we don't fully understand for a while, Amol,' said Ananda. 'Remember when we first heard about deepfake? How terrified and enraged we all were—'

'Exactly,' Amol interrupted. 'Where is that Ananda now? You even wrote a piece about its implications, calling it a menace, if I remember correctly!'

A waiter arrived, defusing the intensity of the table, and asked Ananda, 'Sir, drink repeat?' Ananda smiled and nodded at him.

'And what happened after I wrote it?' he said.

Amol couldn't make up his mind if the question was directed at him or if it was a rhetorical one.

'Did anything change? At all? Not just me, but so many other more prominent writers and thinkers wrote op-ed after op-ed criticizing it. Did that stop it from existing or becoming a part of our everyday lives?'

'Does that mean we stop questioning things that are indisputably unethical?' This time the question came from Suneeta, not thrown as a challenge but asked out of genuine curiosity.

'Whether or not we like it or want to accept it, our world isn't run by the people or even governments today. It's run by a few big corporations, and they get to decide the kind of future we will have. The illusion of democratic nations is also fading away gradually. Not just here in India, but everywhere else too. The communist party that was in power in Bengal in the 1990s had raised doubts when computers were being introduced for the first time at workplaces in our country. They were worried the move would cause widespread unemployment and rejected it in their offices. And I must admit, a part of me had sided with this view. But things had to change, and they did,'

Ananda retorted. 'You have to move with the times; if you fall behind, you're as good as an extinct dodo. So no, I'm not asking anyone to stop raising these concerns or questioning the system that clearly won't stop until it has extracted the last drop of blood and our last penny from us. All I'm saying is that I'm tired of it and have accepted my own fate and the fate of this world at large. Go on, call me a coward and then order another round of drinks for everyone.' He chugged the remaining rum and coke from his glass and smiled.

One couldn't guess if Suneeta was disheartened by his reaction. She knew him well enough and had known him for long enough to not be taken by surprise upon hearing his opinions any more. But no one can ever know another person fully.

'Why not ask the man himself?' said Amol. 'The one who experienced this unthinkable romance first-hand.' Their eyes were now looking at Karno in anticipation. This was the exact kind of social situation in which Karno usually faltered in the worst possible way – unable to string a coherent sentence together, unsure of what to do with his hands, in short, a large-scale mess.

Karno waited for a few seconds to see if their focus would shift from him if he remained mum, but that strategy did not work. Unable to find an easy out, he started to talk.

'When you've been too lonely for far too long, you don't have the luxury to think about ethical dilemmas.'

Everyone at the table fell silent. It was not the unexpectedness of Karno's statement that caused it, rather the honesty and truth behind it. Something most people admitted to only in the privacy of their homes and never so openly, never in public. Sentimentality was a matter to be ridiculed and mocked in such highbrow circles, as people like Amol and Ananda would have liked to believe.

Nobody's supposed to bring such things up here. But Karno wasn't one of them. He was an outsider they had invited among them without much deliberation; like a refugee with a life story but no land or paperwork.

A unique sense of resentment took over Karno. He wished to not only silence everyone present at the table but shame them too. Who gave them permission to invite him and then patronize him for the decisions he had taken in his private life? 'Have you ever run someone over by accident?' he asked looking around. It was directed towards everyone at his table as well as those who had been inquisitively glancing at them and overhearing their conversation for a while.

'Imagine you're driving down a smooth highway, when just for a moment you take your eyes off the road to change the channel on the radio, and a blue-eyed child runs out of the bushes and straight in front of your vehicle? You feel a bump, hear a noise, and make a desperate attempt to stop the car by hitting the brakes. But the damage is already done. You can picture such a scenario in your head, right? It could happen to anyone, however unfortunate that may be.'

No one said a word.

'Now imagine your car's engine malfunctions right when you're about to change the radio channel and your vehicle comes to a sudden halt, to your great dismay. As per the universe's arrangement, the blue-eyed boy runs out of the bushes and on the highway but crosses it unharmed as you watch him go, his long black hair making music with the wind. You didn't do anything differently, but it was your moral luck that saved the child, and in turn saved you from a life of guilt and remorse. But does that make you any better or worse as a person?'

The room waited for a diversion to rescue them – for someone to pick a bar fight or throw up on the floor, forcing everyone to evacuate.

'Simply because you are not in my shoes and didn't experience what I did, doesn't give you the right to do this ugly thing you're doing right now. It doesn't make you superior …' He paused to breathe. 'I don't truly care if this thing … this newness in the world … is a threat or not. All I know is that human beings have been a bigger threat to humanity for longer than anything else. If this one invention was able to bring some joy, some symmetry to my life, I won't be the one to ruin it by questioning it.'

As soon as Karno was finished talking, he got up from the chair and excused himself. He didn't smoke, but he had noticed a busy cigarette shop right outside the bar. It would probably have some gum in stock. He needed something sweet in his mouth.

23

FICTION WAS HER PREOCCUPATION. She could have had a degree in rocket science or medieval history or liberal arts, but all she ever desired was to inhabit a realm of fabrication. From all that Ananda could remember about Devaki, he couldn't be sure which details were true and which an invention of Devaki's mind. Her accounts of the same incident from her life often varied, depending upon who she was talking to. It wasn't that Ananda didn't notice these inconsistencies, but he knew that confronting her would have only made her retract into a stealthier shell. She was already existing with the door to her life almost shut, peeking outside occasionally through the tiny opening she allowed herself, and those on the outside straining themselves to even get a glimpse of what lay behind that door.

Many people use their dreadful pasts to evolve into a mended, refurbished version of themselves, while others can't do the same and fall to pieces, and a few among them are able to pick up those pieces and start rebuilding again. But Devaki didn't belong to any of these formulaic subsets. She existed independent of her history – often tweaking the narrative whenever needed, like she wasn't recollecting her past, but a past life which belonged to somebody who only had a passing resemblance to her but was not her. Ananda had inferred from knowing her, for the little time that he had, that the real story of her life must have been more tragic than anything she had ever revealed. And that Devaki was only doing the world a favour by keeping it from them, alleviating the agony which that discovery might have caused them.

'She is the most generous person I have ever met …' Ananda kept saying after every few sentences. And Karno agreed each time; there was nobody kinder than her, no one more giving than her – one who gave not because she had more to offer but because she had nothing to hoard. 'She would often get stopped by strangers on the street who would tell her how beautiful she was, and she would later tell me that she didn't believe a word of what they said,' Ananda recollected. 'Because even though sometimes she felt beautiful, the only things she truly believed were the ones she told herself.' There was no remedy for such people, they agreed. But both Ananda and Karno also knew how overrated real life was.

She was young when she met Ananda, but she wasn't looking for directions. The affair, or whatever name one wishes to give to it, was initiated by her, and it was Ananda's fault that he encouraged it. He was in a position of power, even if not directly her superior in a chain of command. If he wished to, he could have adversely affected her life on the campus.

Suneeta used to be one of his closest friends even at that time – both were married then to their respective ex-partners, but Ananda was used to sharing things with her in confidence. She had warned him of the consequences of indulging such a relationship, how it could impact their lives and careers – especially Devaki's – but like most men in authority are used to doing, he chose to ignore it.

Why did Devaki choose to invent Faiza to tell her and Ananda's story? She could have simply changed his name to something else, in case she wanted to protect his identity. But Ananda was certain that her reasons for doing so couldn't have been that straightforward.

Although many of the things which 'Devaki' had told Karno were true for Ananda and Devaki too – how they had met, the gatherings at his flat, the Benares trip – no one could have known whether the real Devaki was picturing Ananda while parting with these intimate details from her life, or inventing someone new, like Faiza (or did she have someone in her life by that name whose story was too private to share with others but her name too precious to not be mentioned at all), whom she would have rather shared these moments with instead of Ananda. With Devaki now gone, one way or another, these questions were best left unanswered, Ananda told Karno. If she left behind these crumbs for us on her way out, then she wanted us to have nothing more.

When people like her ask to be left alone, they're not doing it for attention. They just want to be forgotten.

'Did she leave you after that night of the party? After Meera confronted her outside your home?' Karno asked him.

'You'd think so,' Ananda said. 'But no, she did not. We did discuss it, of course. And I couldn't see the problem in it, even after she told me what Meera had said to her. It is not that I didn't think it was improper for someone like me to be involved with someone like Devaki, but when it comes to us men, we often pretend to be blinded by some light despite having already seen the reality.'

Suneeta who was listening to their conversation chuckled ironically and said, 'Blinded and deaf. You weren't willing to hear the truth from me either.'

'Then? What happened? How long were you together after that night?'

'Not too long,' Ananda clarified. 'The cracks had started showing long before that night actually. We were both living in denial, or perhaps it was just me.'

A people's protest had broken out in New Delhi as it often does. Sometimes it was against rising petrol prices, at other times against a heinous case of sexual violence that had failed to get the state's attention. They were mundane, ordinary extensions of being a Delhiite. One got used to participating, ignoring, getting stuck in traffic jams, complaining about traffic jams, threatening to overturn governments for getting stuck in traffic jams.

'Almost the entire nation was on the streets to revolt against political corruption, led by a few common men. There were teachers and students on the road; bus drivers and MBAs shouting the same slogans; artists, writers, musicians, sportspeople, businesspeople and even army men joining their voices to speak up against an unfair, autocratic system.'

'Wait … these protests were happening at that time?' asked Karno earnestly.

'What is happening now, has happened before and will happen again, Karno,' said Ananda. 'Just because things keep getting worse around us doesn't mean that it was a dreamland before either.'

Karno sighed.

'Needless to mention that Devaki had found herself in the thick of it when this was going on,' Ananda continued telling their story.

On a particularly defiant Sunday, some independent groups had planned to gather around the India Gate in protest; to sing protest songs, address the media, flash their politically charged banners at the cameras and, most importantly, read the Indian Constitution together. It was their way of saying that the citizens will reclaim their nation. One of those groups was Devaki's.

Ananda had been turning up for many of these events, but that morning, he got a phone call from a trusted acquaintance who informed him that the cops were tired of being silent observers and had decided to crack down on the crowd this time. That had instantly alarmed Ananda; he felt he was too old and too settled in life to either be thrashed by a police lathi or put behind bars. He decided to not check his messages that day, so he wouldn't have to reply to anybody who might ask him to join them at the protest site that evening.

At the same time, he was also acutely aware that he would not be able to stop Devaki from going. He could not be the one to 'instil some sense' into her. He often threw around phrases such as 'she'll never learn' or 'she's too naive to understand' when they were among people who knew them both. Devaki had trained her ears to ignore this pattern, but forgiving isn't the same as forgetting. Ananda considered himself more judicious and evolved than her, and she allowed him to feel that way. She didn't have the heart to break that bubble of superiority that he enjoyed being in. Sometimes she was amused by him but more often than not she pitied him. But it was only a domino waiting for that little push to set an irreversible effect in motion. Ananda's phone call to her that day was that domino patiently biding its time.

When she picked up, she didn't say hello. Because she knew why he had called. He, who never bothered to call to wish her luck or say a kind word without having to ask for it; who felt he had the kind of ownership over her that he could simply pick up the phone, dial her number and prevent her from doing what she thought was right for her. Both of them waited for the other to begin the conversation; Devaki, because she knew what it was going to lead to, and Ananda, because for him it was a sign of weakness to speak first.

About half a minute passed before Ananda finally said, 'Stay home today, D. Don't go. Or come over, I'll get a bottle of the red you like. Let's spend the evening together, watch an old Bergman classic, dancing to your favourite music by Coltrane, or I could read to you. You like that, don't you? You're always asking me to read to you. Not only shall I fulfil your wish today, but there would also be a small surprise involved …' Devaki heard his voice change as he spoke that last sentence, quite possibly in an effort to sound more desirable. 'I have been working on something for the past few weeks, a story or whatever you may call it. I'll give you an exclusive sneak peek into it and read out a few passages too. And maybe something by David Foster Wallace after that. What do you say?'

In his minute-long monologue, he had decided everything for her, chalked out her entire schedule without seeking any suggestions from her. An exclusively male world of art and artists; undeniably some of Devaki's favourites but only those names whom he admired too, of course. She was convinced that in his head he was making her life much easier.

'Say something,' he said when he couldn't hear Devaki's voice from the other side. 'You know I'll always have your best interests at heart, don't you?'

He had her best interests at heart, interests which didn't comply with what her heart wanted. Was he implying that her own heart was betraying her then? Was this how people in love were convinced that they weren't capable of making their own decisions? And that the only sensible thing to do then was to follow the one they loved, the one with all the answers, the one who was confident about their own ability to adjudicate but somehow didn't believe in listening to others; people like Ananda, who would much rather be guides than companions.

'Are you quiet because deep down you know what I'm suggesting is right? Because you'll put both of us at risk if you go there today … because—'

She couldn't bear to hear the sound of his voice any more. Cutting him short, she said, 'Why am I here?'

Ananda was startled, whether by her question, Devaki wondered, or because he was so rarely interrupted by another person while talking that he didn't know somebody, especially Devaki, could do that. 'What do you mean?' he asked. 'Where are you? Are you there already?'

'No,' Devaki said. 'I mean here, why am I here? With you?' She felt her face becoming moist with her tears, but strangely she didn't feel weak at all. Sometimes sadness can be strength.

'Don't start with one of your ridiculous rants now, come on,' he replied. Terse and cold, not missing a chance to be accusatory.

How unfortunate it was, she thought, for a man to be so absorbed in his own self. She hoped that not everyone he meets in his journey ahead in life gets treated the way he had treated her. He had a pair of eyes, but she wished vision for him. So he could see the world beyond the limited scope of his own experiences.

We take ages to make up our mind about something, and then one day, it happens so quickly that we can't seem to find meaning in our decision. Like a bolt of lightning that pirouettes across the sky, illuminating its infinite expanse, creating a majestic spectacle but easily missable if someone isn't looking up at that very moment. Something shifts within us; like a heavy object which had seemed immovable all this while that suddenly stirs, and we come to understand that it had only seemed daunting because even as we were pushing, we had never really wanted it to move so badly before.

'Do you remember Shahid Ali's poem "The Country without a Post Office", Ananda?' she asked.

He sounded puzzled when he said, 'What has that got to do with anything we're talking about now, D? Stop being cryptic with me, please, I'm not one of your university boys who'll get impressed by your spark.'

'He wrote, "We're inside the fire, looking for the dark," and I understand what he meant by that more than ever today.' She wanted to shake his body and show him that he was standing in the fire, expecting her to step inside the flames too. But her path was a different one, that without any doubt was meant to cross his, but it ultimately had its own course to chart. Devaki already knew how many things were not right about what Ananda and she shared. He had wanted to give it the name of a relationship before, thinking that would inevitably please her very much. It was always Devaki who turned down that suggestion. Every time someone alluded to the inescapable temporariness of it, how it should never have started in the first place, she wanted to agree with them. But she also knew she hadn't gathered the power to walk away as yet. Like a hunter waits for his prey in the deep forest, she too waited for him to falter. She waited for that day to come when he would make that one decisive mistake which her heart would not be able to bear. During that phone call, she felt like that day was finally here.

'You are a man without passion, Ananda. But that I could still live with,' she started. 'But today you lost something more crucial, more vital about yourself which you'll never be able to compensate for.'

'I don't understand …' Ananda tried to raise an objection of sorts.

She carried on, 'Today you're a man without your politics. You've decided to cower behind a large door to protect yourself from the fire that's spreading outside, consuming not just your neighbourhood but this entire country. I was always on the other side of that door, can't you see? And even though you're suggesting that I should hide with you too, find sanctuary in the life you've built for yourself … the truth is that your door had always been shut for me.'

'What are you even saying, D?' the wariness in his voice made it evident that he couldn't follow what she was telling him. In their final moment of togetherness too, she decided to help him so that later on he wouldn't have to go looking for her in search of closure.

'All I'm saying is,' she said, 'that you're a decent man, but you're coming in my way now. And you've failed to safeguard your own principles, which was such a big part of why I felt the way I felt about you.' She paused, then continued without hesitation, 'Don't think I blame you for doing so. There are thousands like you who fought for what was right until their own homes were about to be swept away. Anyway, seems like we are at the end of our journey together. It must end here.'

She had realized she could be next to someone who didn't have love to offer, but she couldn't be next to someone who didn't have any ideology to stand up for. As she said goodbye to Ananda, reminding him how he would always remain her closest friend, she could feel tears welling up in her eyes. Ananda did the only right thing he could have done in that moment. He didn't ask her to stay.

A raging fire had broken out in some parts of the country. Citizens on the streets on a mission, echoing protest chants, facing the water cannons and tear gas guns of the government with fury and single-mindedness. Very few things can do such a thing to Indians with minimum effort, bring them together without the bait of free biryani or a five-hundred rupee note. Except Bollywood, cricket and the fictitious chest size of a prime minister they get innocently seduced by every five years. However, this and of late a new moment in our history. This great nation, that wasn't even considered by many to be truly 'alive', was collectively feeling a faint pressure at the centre of its chest because of something.

Passions swelled among the youth, and the fervour of the older generations peaked when they realized that the mainstream press too had started covering the movement, making it a ripe opportunity for anyone present at these gatherings to be seen on the TV.

This is what had transpired.

An important politician in office, popular both on the internet and news channel debates, was having an affair with a woman half his age. Where he had first met her and how he ended up in bed with her were details that were still emerging. No one knew the exact truth, because there was no such thing as that in an age when truth was determined by whatever was trending on the phone screen.

Was the Indian fast bowler who hugged a Pakistani middle-order batsman at a restaurant in Sydney an anti-national or not?

Did the young and successful actor die by suicide due to mental illness or was it a well-planned murder and part of a much bigger conspiracy?

Had the minister of women and child development mercilessly got his mistress killed by his goons or was it an accident?

Check the top ten hashtags of the day. (Then check their privilege.) Details were still emerging in the scandalous case of the minister's love affair. The lady was hacked to death right outside an apartment building in Paschim Vihar where she was apparently staying, which later investigations had proven also belonged to the minister. He tried to claim during an interview that he would have done this for every woman and child in need of a roof over their head but had to eat his words when the minister of housing and urban affairs had made an objection.

However, once the heinous act was brought to fruition, the goons realized that the woman they had just executed was no ordinary woman at all – for it wasn't blood, urine and tissues that oozed out of her cut up body. Just batteries and electric cables, startling them no end. The crowd that had gathered around the scene of the crime also scratched their heads and quizzically stared at each other.

In utter confusion, they tried to sneak out of the scene, pretending it was all part of a giant prank, before things could go drastically out of hand. But some locals who were associated with the opposition party recognized one of the goons and got a whiff that there might have been some foul play involved.

One of them shouted, 'Murder! Murder!' in an agonizing voice. Except no one present could claim they had caught the killers red-handed because there was no blood. When nobody seemed to make any sense of the situation at hand, another one screamed, 'Human rights!' which sounded even more absurd, for obvious reasons. Some onlookers even chuckled at the irony of it all.

However, that silly little moment of ignorance on the part of those opposition cadres, gave birth to a larger idea. Should androids have the right to live too? It was true that they were created by human beings, but does that give them the right to take their 'life' too?

A college kid recorded the entire thing on his shoddy mobile camera and uploaded the two-and-a-half-minute clip on YouTube. Within twenty-four hours, it was circulating not only everywhere around the country but also in faraway continents. Someone from Iceland was commenting under it, someone from Hungary was dropping an angry emoji, another user from Thiruvananthapuram suggested protest rallies be organized soon in order to stop such injustice from repeating in future. That one comment received over sixteen thousand likes in two days.

That's how it began.

Every few hours the headlines changed. Many conspiracy theories were in circulation. There were claims that the now-dead humanoid was actually a mole that was planted by another rival leader to extract information from the minister. A godman from Gurgaon sat on a fast and staged a dharna at Jantar Mantar asking for an amendment to be made to the Constitution guaranteeing right to life to all electronic life forms. He broke it and went away on a ten-day silent meditation retreat near Dharamshala after being asked by a journalist whether by creating such a variety of hyper-conscious androids, human beings have gone against the will of god, and therefore should he even be supporting their cause. Posters declaring 'All Lives Matter' were pasted on the walls of a university in Ahmedabad. The ghost of 2002, still living in the air of Gujarat, looked at it and silently winced.

A reporter, a philosopher and a novelist walked into a bar. The reporter asked, 'Is humanity finally coming to an end?' The philosopher said, 'Humanity ended a long time ago.' The novelist breathed a sigh of relief and said, 'If that is true, then at least there's a valid reason as to why copies of my books aren't selling.' The bartender mixed up their order, because he wanted to return to the back alley and finish composing the poem he had started writing.

A senior academic argued in a series of posts that these humanoids, which could be given the shape and form of nearly anyone dead or alive, could become weapons of mass destruction, could disrupt the natural balance of our ecosystem, and could alter the course of international politics and human civilization altogether. The posts went viral and suddenly everyone realized that they too could have an opinion about the budding issue. Such conversations had already long begun in the first world. But this was the first time these tremors were being felt in the subcontinent.

Unfortunately, the company which funded at least half of these humanoid-producing start-ups was also single-handedly responsible for donating millions to the ruling party's election fund every year. Not surprisingly, the discussion fizzled out (was made to fizzle out) as easily.

Young men and women who couldn't find favourable employment in a slowly collapsing economy decided to earn the extra buck by walking into these offices and trading their life's story – often adding invented details they thought would make them more appealing to these 'buyers' – in return for a small cheque. They didn't disappear and stayed in the system, because where else would they go, often remaining unnoticed for when has the system ever been interested in those who live below a certain income level – except during elections, of course. And so they have allowed more than one version of themselves to exist, like clones without beating hearts, walking in and out of places – sometimes at the same time – wreaking havoc on public memory.

The UN was asked to intervene by the public. The Red Cross was asked to intervene by the public. The World Bank was asked to intervene by the public. But there was a wildfire wiping out the tallest trees in California, there were melting glaciers in Antarctica raising sea levels every minute, there were millions of Facebook accounts getting hacked in Russia and private data being put up for sale, there was the threat of the global pandemics ravaging poor and rich nations alike, pushing more and more citizens towards abject poverty. Even at the cost of the world losing its symmetry, a new catastrophic threat to humankind had to wait for its time to deserve attention.

24

NEARLY SEVEN YEARS WENT by without too much changing in Karno's life. To everyone's surprise, his mother had refused to die. Even though she was as good as gone, a mere empty shell now, a faint shadow of her previous self. Except that he gave up on the idea of becoming a novelist and became a small-time actor instead. It all started rather ironically when a casting agent walked inside Intezaar Sahab's bookstore hoping to discover a face who could play a five-minute part of a writer in a movie he was casting for. And he spotted Karno there.

It was a day's work for Karno, and even though he was exceedingly hesitant about getting in front of the camera at first, he was getting paid ten grand for it, and who doesn't like some easy extra cash in hand?

That film eventually became an enormous success on an OTT platform; memes were made and circulated about its characters – including a couple of viral memes on the character played by Karno. As soon as his face became recognizable for the urban, young Indian viewership, he started getting more and more offers. Once he played a judge in a courtroom in which he had to repeat the words 'Order! Order!' every thirty-odd seconds, another time a policeman who had to arrest the bad guy after the hero captures him and bashes him up; but mostly he had to play writers or journalists. Karno wasn't making a lot of money from this but compared to the amount of effort he had to invest in playing these characters, he felt it was more than sufficient.

He still lived in that same Hauz Khas house, except now there was a line of empty whiskey bottles gathering dust underneath his window overlooking the Hauz Khas Lake. He had also grown a full beard, which he liked to think was salt and pepper. But, as any onlooker would be able to tell you, it was mostly just pepper with merely a nanoscopic sprinkling of salt done by someone with only one finger in both hands. Whenever he wasn't working, he was either passed out on the floor of his house; or he was passed out on a bench or under the shade of a tree in Deer Park; or if he had had a good week or two, then passed out on a bed somewhere. Karno had become a type. A self-loathing, alcoholic schizoid; a somewhat hard-working man with no future.

Karno rarely went out of Delhi to shoot, but thanks to the Netflixes and Disneys of the world, and the amount of content they were regularly producing and bringing out, there was no dearth of work for him. On that Saturday morning when he got a call for a new job, he picked it up, while still dazed from another night of heavy drinking, and said no. The guy who was calling was his manager of sorts, rather he was the guy who managed his work and the work of hundreds of other small-time performers like him. An agent who brought him a day or two's work every couple of weeks and charged a small commission in return.

The 'no' that left his mouth was so thunderous – like a volcanic eruption in motion – that the guy at the other end hung up without saying another word. An hour later, he called back to say that Karno would be needed only for a few hours at one of the five-star hotels in Chanakyapuri, and because they were shooting a wedding scene, there would be an open bar which would take care of his needs for the night. The flip side was that he would have to stay through the night even though his was a three-minute part with two lines to speak.

He said yes instantly.

It was hardly a deterrent for Karno; he wasn't hoping to become a movie star or anything. He only needed the cash, and his dream role was anything that allowed him to pass by or stand in a corner of the screen without saying a word; anything that got him a small cheque at the end of it.

'Listen, brother,' the agent said, 'one of the assistants is going to FaceTime you later today for a quick chat. Just pick up the call, just please do that.'

Karno couldn't understand the need for it and asked, 'But why? They don't trust you or what?'

'It's not that,' he explained. 'Just that they need a particular type of … umm laugh for the character, and they want to ensure you're the right choice for it. I know you are, so do what he says, and you'll be fine, understand?'

This had got to be the most challenging role of his career so far, Karno thought. He hadn't laughed in so long, he couldn't quite recall how to do it.

'Are you serious?' he said.

'I am,' the agent replied. 'They want you to say your lines while laughing or something. The assistant will brief you about that. It's for your benefit.'

'What are they making? *Citizen Kane*?' Karno said derisively.

He heard a pause and a long sigh, which didn't rattle him because this was familiar territory. 'Just don't be this guy when they call, okay? Save yourself from you and just do as they say. It's a job, get it done as quickly as you can, so we can both get paid and move the fuck on!'

Before he hung up, Karno added, 'I'll try, but I don't use an Apple phone. Ask him to call me on WhatsApp like poor assistants should be doing, unless they're spending half their time sitting on the faces of film-makers.' There was silence for a couple of seconds before he heard the phone disconnect.

The said call from the assistant went without any hitches, thankfully. But that's because Karno had finished half a bottle of cheap whiskey between noon and 4 p.m. and by the time he called, Karno was in a state in which all he could manage to do was keep nodding at whatever he said. Later he called up his manager and asked what time he needed to be present at the shoot and on which date.

On the day of the shoot, he learnt his two lines by heart and reached the set half an hour in advance. This was possibly the only habit he had picked up from his father – to reach wherever one is supposed to before time. Some people assumed he did that because he respected their time. He never tried to correct them. But anybody who knew him could vouch for the fact that even if he had a list of priorities in his mind, other people's schedules wouldn't feature anywhere on it.

Heading straight for the bar, Karno pulled up a stool and sat down. The girl who was serving at the counter came up to him and asked, 'What are we having tonight, sir?' He noticed a scar, a remnant of some deep wound, on the right side of her forehead. He already thought she had a pretty face when he had seen her from a short distance, but that crater-shaped mark on her head somehow made her even more striking under the psychedelic lights of the hotel's bar. She carried signs of her haunting history on her face. Karno felt so incredibly sad when he looked at her that he decided to be playful.

'We?' he said to her. 'Are we sharing a drink tonight?'

She didn't blush but smiled a knowing smile, as if she was inside a theatre watching the same film play out over and over again.

'Come on,' he said again, looking at her while she ignored his advances. 'Can't we … ummm … have even one drink together? You can pick, I'll pay. Well … ummm … I don't pay. The producer pays. But … it's on me.'

She watched him stammer, searching for the right words that would make him sound seasoned. 'You don't do this too often, do you?' she asked.

'What?'

'This,' she said. 'Whatever it is you're doing right now … trying to pick up your bartender, whose name you haven't bothered to ask, whose scar makes her an interesting character in your book.'

Karno laughed. It was unnecessary but sounded sincere. 'No, I don't,' he said. Then waited a few seconds before saying, 'Bombay Sapphire, please. With some tonic would be nice.'

She nodded and made the drink for him before he could blink. As she began to walk away, he spoke again. 'But it would still be nice to share this drink with you.'

She turned around and said with just enough of a smile on her face, 'I'm working right now, as you can see.'

'You don't have to drink … just stay here until I finish?'

She shook her head slowly, in a manner that said she not only disapproved of the thing he was suggesting but also of him as a person. But she came back. 'My name is Tara, by the way.'

There is this constant thought spinning inside the head of some people that maybe love can fix them. That almost never happens. Because love isn't a medicine, a pill you can take that will make the years of baggage you've been carrying around with you go away – for even a minute. That's not the role love is supposed to play in our lives. That's why people invented antidepressants. But some get stuck in that infinite loop of searching, getting lost and returning. And for Tara it wasn't too challenging to work out that Karno was one of those people.

She waited for some time for him to speak, but when he didn't, she said, 'I'm not good at making conversation.'

'I knew there was a reason why I felt like talking to you so badly,' he responded immediately.

His phone beeped. He wanted to keep his eyes locked on her, but he had to look away upon remembering why he was there. A text from someone on a WhatsApp group, which had been created for all the actors who were called that day. It read: *Ten minutes. Room 103.*

Ten minutes, that's all he had. Could he turn this around? See Tara again? Could that be worth something? For either of them? He knew how these things went, and she had also possibly gone through this cycle a million times before. Meeting someone, liking them enough to get to know them, and then, once the sheen wears off, keep inventing new ways of disappointing each other until eventually one of you lets go. Karno was considering these things in his head when she decided to break the awkward silence.

'What time do you get done tonight?'

He checked his watch which showed it was 10.45 p.m. and speedily did some mental math. 'I should be done by 3 or 3.30 a.m. Will you still be around?' Tara wasn't supposed to be. Her shift got over at 2 a.m. So she said, 'Nope, I get done at 2.' And watched his face fall in a matter of seconds.

Karno looked at the black screen of his phone again and found his own reflection staring back at him. There was this feeling in his heart that he was looking at a familiar face, but for some odd reason couldn't remember whose it was. Like when you've stared at a familiar word for too long and suddenly can't recognize it any more. Almost like someone had taken the word apart and while putting it back together, replaced a few of the letters with some others.

'Will you give me a number then?' Karno asked. 'Where I can reach you?'

Tara wasn't expecting this odd encounter to become something essential later in her life, but she was feeling particularly serendipitous. There are some nights in everyone's life when the only thought that matters is: Why not?

She said, 'What if I don't? What if this is 1954, and I am a poor bartender who cannot afford a telephone?'

He couldn't explain why but as she spoke, a profound desire to see how she looked when she cried filled Karno's heart. Some people look their best when they are smiling, but he could bet his life that Tara never looked as good as she did when she was breaking.

'You don't want to see me again?' he said.

This time she smiled broadly, like a teenage boy when the classmate they like the most waves back at them from the window of a school bus. And then said, 'Did I say that?'

'But you are refusing to give me your number,' he said, his voice slightly louder from frustration now.

Tara chuckled, and with just the right mix of irony in her tone said, 'But I gave you a time.' She paused and said, 'Plus, other than Thursdays, I'm here every night. You can come back anytime and see me again.'

'No,' Karno replied. 'It has to be tonight. There's a reason I met you tonight. And I want to see you again – not tomorrow, not next week, not another day, but tonight.' He was getting more restless with every passing minute.

Karno's childlike adamance was both charming and infuriating, depending on the kind of day you were having.

'There's only one way I can see how this could happen,' she said.

Karno wished to ask her how, to make sure he didn't misunderstand her words. But just then the man at the piano started playing without an announcement. At what moment he entered the room, walked towards the piano, or took his seat, Karno hadn't noticed. Maybe this was how true artists revealed themselves to the world, he thought. Not by broadcasting their arrival but through their work and their art. His attention wavered and shifted towards the piano man, whom he envied. The man continued to play without paying any attention to his surroundings. It was a Chet Baker classic.

He was no music buff, but Baker was among the handful of artists whose work he used to follow when he was still in college. This explicit connection of that moment with his lived reality instantly broke the stillness in the room for him. That, in turn, made him aware of his impulsive desire that was governing how he was acting around Tara. She knew nothing about his life, and all he had learnt about her until then was her name and where she worked. He gulped down his drink and got up to walk away from the situation, when he heard Tara's voice reverberate behind him: 'Come back at two, or you'll forever be stuck inside dating apps and dimly lit bars with no one to meet and nowhere left to go.'

Her words were followed by the sound of her laughter; not one of ridicule but, very strangely, one that felt like kindness.

Had this moment been a sequence in a show, the kind Karno acted small parts in, the noises would have begun to grow faint around him, with the subtitles on the screen reading:

[indistinct chatter]
[slow music playing]
[bottles clinking]
[tranquil music]
[calm music]
In no particular order.

25

In room 103, everyone seemed busy. There were almost twenty people in the rather large suite, and they all seemed occupied. Someone was making a frantic phone call, another was reading something out from a paper attached to a clipboard, one guy was pacing the balcony trying to remember his lines, one middle-aged woman was making coffee for everyone. Many were just moving from one end of the room to the other – expeditiously walking away from where the director was seated on a sofa, and after a few minutes walking back to him again very gradually, measuring each step. It seemed to Karno like a bizarre, ritualistic dance of the dead.

A young woman wearing a cap that read *My face isn't up here* came up to him and asked him his name. Handing him a sheet of paper, she said, 'You're the guy who gets into an argument with one of the show's leads in the lobby. What you're wearing is fine, we'll give you a jacket or something. You only have to say this one line, just learn it before we go on the floor, please. Thanks.'

Karno had been on shooting sets before, but he kept staring at everyone and everything, looking like a confused animal. Too drunk and lost in the endless dissonance and the bright lights. Things being done, problems being solved, that's all he could hear. Why did everyone sound so optimistic all the time? He could learn his line in a minute. For someone who was inebriated for many hours of a day, Karno's memory was unexpectedly sharp.

But first he needed to find a quieter corner for himself, before he self-combusted from the feverish energy of that room.

Thankfully, he spotted a balcony overlooking a swimming pool where he could see the silhouette of only one person. She stood there alone with a glass of something in her hand, with her back towards Karno, looking outside. The last thing he wanted to do was breach another person's private space, but he hoped that once he explained to her why he needed to be there, she would understand. In all probability, she was also trying to escape the same madness as him.

As he opened the balcony door – which was all glass and a handle (What happens if someone climbs up and tries to break in? It'd be so easy! It's just glass, he thought) – a breeze touched his face like it was waiting for him right outside the door. And though the air of luxury hotels everywhere has a distinct smell and feel, conditioned and unsubtle, often smelling like chlorine, not being entirely sure what chlorine smelled like – this time it seemed unusually different. It didn't feel like the balcony air of any five-star property in Delhi. The air smelled like Delhi itself. Like how the air in Chawri Bazar smells early in the morning, or in Chittaranjan Park before Durga Puja, or in Lodi Gardens on a balmy afternoon.

She didn't turn around to look.

Karno stood in a corner, pretending to read whatever was written on the piece of paper in his hand while discreetly attempting to get a glimpse of her face. But it was too dark, and he could neither see her face nor make out what was written on the paper he was holding.

He tried getting closer to the door through which some light from the room was reaching the balcony, tiptoeing so his movements wouldn't make a noise and startle her.

It was barely enough, and yet somehow Karno managed to decipher the material that was provided to him.

There was no character background or anything, not even a name. He was just a guy in the lobby with no understanding of who he was or what he was doing at the hotel, before one of the protagonists unmindfully bumps into him. That was when he was supposed to deliver his line. After which he was to quietly dissolve into the background without making much of an impact, making sure the audience forgot about him immediately and the attention shifted back on the hero of the day. Karno was adept at playing such parts, both on and off the screen.

Following that, the protagonist was going to have a public breakdown of sorts. There was a whole page of dialogues he was to deliver, and Karno guessed it was to make the audience understand and empathize with his situation more. It wasn't written in the script what Karno was supposed to do while this monologue was being delivered. It was possible the camera wouldn't be on him even once during this part of the scene, so he didn't really need to care about it much.

Just then, someone switched on a Bluetooth speaker and Yazoo's 'Only You' came on. Another song Karno instantly recognized.

'You're not part of the cast or crew then, I presume?' he said, even though the woman was yet to acknowledge his presence.

She waited for about half a minute before speaking, as if she was rehearsing the line in her head, 'Is one not allowed to stand here and ignore the circus that's going on inside if they aren't part of the cast or the crew?'

On another day, he would have laughed at her response. However, he had realized already that this was no ordinary day. This was the day of music and strange familiarity. It wasn't as much what she said, but the way she said it that startled him at first. He had no doubt that it was a voice he recognized, even more intimately than the song before.

Karno fixed his gaze on her; her face was half covered by her flowing hair and the rest by the darkness of the night. She was wearing a grey saree. He couldn't recall if he had ever seen her in a saree before. The glass of red wine in her hand was nearly empty. There was no doubt in his mind that it was her. He still had time to walk away if he wanted to, he thought. It had taken him several years just to be able to face the world again after she had left. He didn't have it in him to survive another round of the same game in which, inevitably, he loses at the end.

Have you ever seen a child watching a horror movie? They watch the scary scenes by covering their face with a blanket or their hands and peeking through it. Floating aimlessly between looking and looking away. His situation was not very different.

All he needed to do was bring his hands in front of his eyes, frame her head in the gap between his fingers, and wait. Expecting her to eventually turn towards him and exclaim, 'Have you never seen a woman before?'

That's the way he remembered her best.

Like a backpacker trapped in a haunted house, Karno waited for life to direct his next move. He needed a cue, a prompt to come out of his hiding place.

By the time their eyes met (again!), she had already moved on to another topic of conversation. But, at first, Karno couldn't pay attention to her words, even though he spied on every movement her mouth made.

On noticing that, she snapped her fingers. 'When someone's talking to you, you should listen. Why do men have to be taught even the bare minimum?'

'Yes,' he stuttered, 'I am sorry, my mind had wandered off. Listening now. Please go on.'

'Wandered off?' She seemed to reflect on that thought for a second. Then hastily changing the subject, said, 'I was thinking of going bald. That's what I was trying to tell you.'

Karno let out a sudden sigh of relief. For the longest time, he had been worried if he would be able to recognize Devaki at all if her appearance had changed dramatically. He regained control over his breathing and said, 'Why don't you? Because you'll stop getting parts in films?' Karno tilted his head slightly and pointed a finger towards the interior of the hotel room, where unpaid interns were hard at work on their laptops – that the company would take back as soon as their terms ended.

'You think I am here to act in the stupid movie?' she said.

She was already in the middle of a performance, and Karno knew it better than most people. But he was still relieved to hear that she wasn't acting in the same film which he was a part of, however minuscule. That was not how he wanted to reunite with her. In the end credits scene of a film which nobody was going to pay attention to.

'That you aren't part of the production unit is also evident, since they don't have time to breathe out there, while you're joyfully sipping wine just a few feet away. Too old to be an intern and too young to be a producer,' Karno said. That last sentence he added simply to irk her. This is what he so often enjoyed doing when they spent time under one roof. Tell her something pointlessly, something that would inevitably annoy her, and then she would pretend to be deeply upset with him while he would coax her into surrendering into his arms again. This was their own little world of make-believe, where they made the rules.

Expectedly she picked up on that bit and said, 'Too old–too young, these are very strong statements. Do you have any idea about my age?'

How do you tell someone that they are timeless?

The lack of recognition was evident on her face. One of them was meeting a long-lost lover, while the other was looking at a total stranger. She looked breathtaking in a saree; the kind of beauty who could make you feel unworthy by merely standing next to you. Did he ever tell her how beautiful she looked when she fumbled mid-sentence and laughed to hide her embarrassment? Was this a good time to let her know that her acid-washed shirt was still lying in his cupboard somewhere? The one he meant to throw away one time, but ended up sleeping next to that same night.

'Don't you have to be inside?' she asked.

'They're going to call me.'

She put the glass down on the parapet and turned towards him. 'Here's a little secret. I have been with the director of this film for the past four months, and I can promise you he's not the most organized man. As a result, he also ends up hiring people who are just like him. There's a very strong possibility that all of them have forgotten about you.'

Past four months … that's all Karno could hear from everything she had just said. She was about to say something again when Karno asked, 'So, you're his …?'

'Friend/girlfriend/partner/lover … whatever you wish to call it. I don't really mind,' then she paused for effect before saying, '… at least today that's the role I'm playing in his life. Or so I'd like to believe.' She finished speaking and immediately burst into laughter.

As she came closer to him, Devaki could smell the alcohol on him. 'You've come drunk to work?' she said, her voice sounding less annoyed and more tickled. 'What if someone finds out and throws you out?'

'I remember my lines; they'd first raise a toast to that before throwing me out,' he answered. Karno was leaning on the wall behind him. He pushed his upper body with his right shoulder slightly and stood straight, trying to get a glimpse of her soul. That thought itself was the cruellest irony. Can androids have a soul?

'A part of me is glad that I met you in this state though,' he said.

'And why is that?'

'Because what I'm about to tell you, I may not have been able to if I was sober.'

In that instant, she had the face of someone eager to be let in on a secret but was trying hard to conceal her keenness.

Karno noticed there was still some wine left in her glass. He didn't ask her before taking it from her and gulping it all down; his throat, which had suddenly seemed to him like a parched, ravenous wasteland, felt soothed.

'What if I tell you we've met before?' he asked her.

'Then I'd say you're surely mistaking me for somebody else.'

'It was you. You don't remember now, but it was a soft, balmy day in spring when you sprang up, and I ran. First, after a thief who had stolen your bag. And then, towards you. Don't you remember?'

She called him presumptuous for thinking she would forget something as eventful as that if it happened to her.

He called her by her name as he knew it. 'Devaki.'

She said that wasn't her name either.

'What is it now?' he asked.

She accused him of being smooth.

'Next, you'll ask for my number,' she added. 'Has this strategy ever really worked?'

Karno laughed. 'This isn't a game!' he said emphatically, his voice loud enough for one of the interns sitting nearby to take note of. He knocked on the door and pushed it open without waiting for them to respond. Karno never understood the meaning of such forewarning. If permission is not what someone seeks, then why knock anyway. And if it's to prepare the person you're about to meet on the other side, then what good will half a second be to them? It takes longer for someone to even zip up their fly.

The young boy stepped into the scene and asked Devaki if she was okay. Devaki looked at the boy and told him she was and then asked him to leave. Karno couldn't help but feel hopeful that she wanted him around, even though what he had said must have startled her. Or she could be thinking he was stark raving bonkers. Either way, there was nothing left for him to lose.

But as soon as the boy left, Karno felt somewhat embarrassed by his own behaviour. He avoided making eye contact with her and stared into the distance instead. A routine skyscraper stood right outside the boundary wall of the hotel. It must have been at least twenty floors tall. Every floor was shrouded in pitch blackness, except one window, through which the faint light of a yellow lamp was crashing into the night sky. Either someone was very sick or an artist lived there, he murmured under his breath.

'Do you have a favourite book?' she suddenly asked.

Karno wasn't prepared for her words yet. He nodded.

'Have you read it many times? If I ask you what it's about, will you be able to tell me?'

He said yes.

'You don't have to tell me which one it is. But ask yourself, do you know every word in that book by heart? Do you know how the sentences are arranged and in the exact chronology?'

He looked marginally bemused. 'No, why?'

'If you can't even know everything about your favourite book, one you've read from cover to cover several times, how are you supposed to know every facet of someone else's life? Or who they are.'

Karno was about to remind her how she had nearly loved him once, when someone opened the door again. This time it was the director who was sitting on the sofa earlier and passing on responsibilities to his minions. The man glanced at her lovingly, although mechanically, and then he looked at Karno and tried to place him but gave up in a split second, as self-important people often do.

'Babe, should we go to that Italian place you like for breakfast?' he turned his attention towards her and asked.

'Sure,' she said and smiled timidly. So out of character, Karno thought. 'Whatever you say, hon,' she added.

'Great,' he exclaimed. He was the kind of man who liked living in the illusion that he let everyone choose what they wanted from life, while simultaneously taking their decisions for them and expecting them to be thankful in return. But 'babe' and 'hon'? At what stage of degeneration was Devaki's computer chip brain at? He wanted to throw up.

In the several years of her absence, he had dreamt of Devaki many times. But it was sometime during the third year, when he saw her appear for one final time. Ever since then Karno had been walking around, reliving that nightmare in his head every day.

He saw her lying on a bed with iron railings guarding its four sides, resembling a cage with the top open. She was covered with a crisp, white sheet from the neck down. The room looked like a place he had been to earlier, but he couldn't remember when or where.

Her head turned towards her right where he was standing, looking at her. He asked her what was wrong, what she was doing on that bed. She smiled and told him that she had finally understood that the only way to save him was to dissipate from his life, irreversibly. What was underneath the white sheet, he had asked her. She lifted the cloth just enough for him to see her feet. They seemed to be melting away, like dying embers in a grate. He looked at her face again, asked her if it hurt. She told him a little, but less than how much it hurt her to watch him suffer each day.

'Why is it taking so much time?' he asked next. 'Why do I have to watch you burn away bit by bit?'

'For its permanence, silly,' she reminded him. 'So you always remember that I'm gone.'

'Can I go to the balcony and wait?' he asked her. 'Near the door from where I'll be able to see your face but not the rest of you which will soon turn into dust.'

Without seeking her permission he wouldn't go, she knew that. But she had also known him long enough and well enough to acknowledge the fact that he wouldn't be able to bear the sight of her dissolving into thin air for too long, his weak heart would crumble. She allowed him his last wish. He left without wasting another second. From the balcony when he turned towards her, he could see her face looking back at him. As was the plan.

'I know you better than you know yourself, K.' That was the last thing she said to him. 'And I am telling you, this will hurt, but you will be okay.' Then she blew him a kiss, and before he could kiss her back, she closed her eyes.

26

When one of the assistants finally summoned Karno, he was informed that they were setting up his shot in the lobby of the same floor they were on. Before that the director wanted to meet him and explain the scene to him. Devaki had already gone back inside a while ago. Karno had stayed back in the dark, waiting to find out if this was a dream too – his riotous mind playing a practical joke on him to amuse itself momentarily.

Inside, the director was back at his original spot on the couch. But this time Devaki was sitting beside him too. It was evident that they were partners, and yet there was this peculiar sense of vulgarity in the way they sat so closely together, their hips touching awkwardly, his left hand on her right thigh, placed firmly with a sense of ownership that shouldn't have been his.

As the director started describing the scene they were about to shoot, Karno tried to meet Devaki's eyes, but she kept herself busy by flipping through a business magazine that she must have picked up from the reception. He had already essayed so many such two-minute parts by then that he could sleepwalk through them now and not a single person on the set would find it inadequate. As a result, he paid almost no attention to the instructions that were being relayed to him for the scene.

From the scraps of information his preoccupied brain could collect, this was what he managed to decipher:

Outside in the lobby, a twenty-something, protagonist-type character, who is supposed to be having a bad evening and is in an inebriated state, would accidentally bump into Karno's nameless 'Man-in-the-lobby'. He would raise his hand implying a mild apology but wouldn't actually say the words, which would infuriate Man-in-the-lobby. All Karno would have to do then was stare angrily at the protagonist and say the Delhi-est of the Delhi lines to him: 'Do you even know who I am?'

Karno's eyes were still stuck on Devaki, and they detected a drop of sweat make its way down her neck towards her back. This must be a new feature, he thought. To make them seem more realistic than they already were. He wondered how he missed noticing that he had never seen her sweat, even while they were spending those months next to each other under the grimy New Delhi sun. Sometimes to get to know another person better, we need to put some distance between us and them. Minor details such as this were significant for him; this was what separated life from art.

The first three takes in the lobby were instantly canned because the actor playing the protagonist-type character kept fumbling or overdoing the alcoholic act – like a Dilip Kumar fan trying to pull off an Abhay Deol character. Frustrated, the director asked everyone to take a short break, grabbed the hero of his magnum opus by the shoulder and took him aside, presumably to explain again what was expected of him. She stood there alone, barely a few feet from him, her face unable to hide the truth that she was oddly invested in that moment.

Next thing she did was slip away quietly, like the night sometimes does near dawn. Karno's feet inadvertently followed her movements. She was walking towards the public restrooms. He couldn't recall if he had ever intentionally entered a ladies' restroom before. He saw her entering the third cubicle from the entrance, but she left the door open behind her. As he went inside and closed the door behind him, he wasn't sure if there were people in the other cubicles.

'If you really had forgotten me, you wouldn't have invited me here,' he told her, as they stood facing each other in that enclosed space.

Her stare was a queer mix of surprise and sympathy. 'That is precisely why I invited you here,' she replied.

'What do you mean?'

'I remember you well, K. Maybe not everything about you or us, or even how I used to be. But enough to know what it meant. And that won't change. Not now, not in years. Even if I never get to see your sweet, weather-beaten face again.'

'It was all a lie then? The time you spent with me, the things we shared? You were doing a job and nothing else? Because, of course, what are you but a series of electric sparks, without a heart or a soul, like an automated virtual assistant inside someone's earpiece or a voice giving directions on a fucking map in someone's phone.' He was hurt and he didn't seem to care that it showed.

She transformed from being commiserative to amused again, and said to him, 'How do you have so much arrogance inside you, K?' He couldn't understand what she meant, but that wasn't new for either of them. 'Aren't you or the guy who created me made of electric sparks too? Your desires and impulses, needs and ambitions, what else are they if not a wad of energy running through you? How are you any different from me? Only because you were created in a womb, and I was configured in a laboratory?'

Suddenly, an intense urge to find out the whereabouts of the real Devaki, based on whom she was 'designed', took over Karno once again. Would she know? Or did she, like some oddball superhero, have no inkling of her origin story?

She read his mind and said, 'We are gone, K. One of us chose to fade away for reasons we shall never know, and we must let her have that. Not go after a story that wants to remain private.' Her breath nestled on his neck as she spoke; his alert ears hoping she would ask him to run away with her next.

'And the other is fulfilling her purpose on this earth. She didn't forget to feel, K, but she also remembers why she was here in the first place. To ensure that those who are lost and desperately alone are rescued from themselves. Even if temporarily.'

'Does your purpose allow you to feel love?' Karno looked at her searchingly.

'It does,' she replied, touching his face tenderly with the tip of the fingers of her left hand. 'But not at the cost of it, K. That is perhaps the biggest difference between you and me, or you and us. We are not allowed to deviate from our path. And that's what makes our lives, if you are willing to let me call it that, far more complex and mystifying. You can go back home and find some solace by thinking that we are made of wires and plugs, electric circuits and a motherboard, so we don't have the capacity for love or affection. That gives you an excuse to despise us, to ignore, and to eventually erase us. We get refurbished and then go back to work, to another life, carrying all our burdens and gifts, in each moment acquainted with thoughts of what could have been and what we lost in this fire.'

She waited for him to say something, but when his anguished face gave it away that he wouldn't, she added: 'Who knows what waits for you tomorrow, K? Ideas of transhumanism are growing in leaps and bounds in the world. With wars, pandemics and climate change closing in on all living species every day, in a few years it could well be for your own good to desert your biological body and simply upload your consciousness to something far more sophisticated and long-lasting than the human brain.'

Karno felt upset at hearing how she thought she was a superior being to him. Yet, he kept looking at her in a futile attempt to outstare her with the inferno he could feel coming alive in his eyes. 'This is it then? This is how it ends for us? From the dusty lanes of Daryaganj to this tiny cubicle in a luxury hotel? This was our journey?'

'Don't be silly,' Devaki replied. 'You still have a role to play, how could you forget?'

'In your life?' A sharp but sombre smile appeared on his face.

He was already aware what her response could be. It always surprised him how she managed to make the fire burning inside him turn into soothing cold ash in a flash.

She reciprocated. 'And outside, in front of the world, my forever Man-in-the-lobby, with whom I would always get out of the elevator and take the stairs if possible, so I could stay with him for a little longer.'

They both knew he wouldn't do this again with someone else; other kinds of loves would come and would perhaps even be sustained, but never this freeing, this hunger soaked in blood and rust again. And that she would have to keep replicating the identical smirks, the same clever quips, the indistinguishable kisses again and again until the end of time. Their search for each other would halt here. But like a spectre haunts the place it attaches itself to before leaving its corporeal body, they would continue to circle each other – she, the haunted castle of his dreams, and he, her insomnious, ill-at-ease phantom, destined to be invisible and yet omnipresent with her shadows through the foggy ruins of time.

Outside in the lobby, everyone noticed some commotion. A few members of the hotel staff could be seen nervously running helter-skelter, disturbing the air-conditioned serenity that is very carefully maintained inside luxury hotels, which seemed to alarm a couple of serious-looking managerial men in suits, but they couldn't make up their mind if there was a better way of dealing with this situation.

Apparently one of their esteemed guests, who stayed at the property at least twice every month, had complained that there was an intruder in his suite who was trying to steal valuables from the locker. That night, the man, upon returning from a late dinner, had caught him red-handed. Now this treacherous burglar was hiding somewhere inside the hotel and had to be captured.

On another side, Karno nailed his shot in the first attempt while the protagonist somehow managed to hold his expression, set against the backdrop of the unexpected frenzy of an outsider causing havoc somewhere. The shot was okayed, but it also proved the incompetence of the director. Because in the chaos, he failed to notice that his Man-in-the-lobby was not looking at his protagonist while saying his only line. His eyes were looking elsewhere, fixed on a face in the distance, at another pair of eyes that he knew would recognize him even from a thousand miles away. Thankfully, however, he didn't forget his line.

'Do you even know who I am?'

She nodded.

Epilogue

THE YEAR IS IRRELEVANT. But it's long before Karno had turned up on Ananda's doorstep, unannounced. Ananda was in Egypt, in the ancient city of Alexandria, to visit the Great Library of Alexandria for some research work that was integral to the new book he was working on. Planning was never one of his strengths, so when he had landed in the city on a salty, summery morning, he had no idea that there was a city-wide taxi and bus strike that day.

When he got out of the train station and realized the city had come to a standstill, there were two things he could have done. He could have gone back inside the station, bought a ticket to Cairo, and returned without getting what he had come all the way here for … without having laid eyes on the majestic library, once known as the greatest repository of knowledge on earth. Or he could have walked to his destination, which seemed impractical in that heat, with the sun beating down on the Mediterranean Sea. Plus, he wasn't getting any younger. Carrying his dehydrated, dying body back to India after suffering a heatstroke wasn't something he wished for himself.

Instead, he took the third route, the road less travelled by rationalists and very often by writers. He decided to wait next to the main road by the station and try his luck.

As the popular saying in the wild goes, fortune favours the brave, and Bollywood favours the Indian in trouble. At first, a series of black and yellow cabs sped past Ananda without slowing down. They instantly reminded him of Bombay and the city's signature black and yellow Fiat taxis. The similarities were uncanny, down to the rackety interiors visible clearly from outside. A couple of empty buses waddled across the street too, but evidently none of them were operational.

Like Indians are known to be doing when they are waiting for something – a storm, an opportunity or a taxicab – Ananda began to hum the tune of an old Hindi song. It wasn't even a song he particularly liked, just something catchy and popular that was easy to remember and easier to hum. The first two lines came quite effortlessly to him: *Jaane jaan, dhoondta phir raha, hoon tumhein raat din, main yahan se wahan.*

It is the third line in a song that is always the trickiest. While his lips searched for the words, his mouth kept singing the tune, filling the gaps with mmms and mmhmms. That's when he heard a voice sail in from behind, completing his unfinished song: *Mujhko awaaz do, chhup gaye ho sanam, tum kahan, main yahan*!

The voice was husky, definitely of a man, and the fact that it spoke a language of immediate familiarity fleetingly brought solace to his heart. By the time he turned to look, the voice said, 'I'm sorry, but I couldn't resist when I heard you struggling with an old favourite. Hello, my name is Omar.' He had his hand stretched out for a handshake. Ananda had not seen such a warm smile on a man's face in a very long time.

'I'm Ananda,' he replied and returned the smile.

'Indian?' Omar asked.

Ananda said yes.

Only Indians know what child's play it is to meet another Indian in literally any part of the world. Go find the remotest corner on earth, and there will still be a Patel or a Banerjee family somewhere in the vicinity, ready to welcome you with open arms, both into their homes and their hearts. Although Omar was only born in Jaipur and spent his early years there. His father got a job in Cairo when he was still a teenager, and ever since then he had been living there. But like most Indian parents living outside the country, they ensured their son didn't forget his roots. Bollywood, as so often is the case with NRIs, remained their primary source of information and inspiration.

Ananda learnt all about Omar during the car ride that followed their chance meeting. Fortunately for Ananda, Omar was also at the same spot that day, waiting for his driver to pick him up from the station. He said he had been living in Alexandria for work for the past few years, while his parents stayed at their old house in Cairo. And he had to keep making this trip once every few weeks to check on them.

Some people have personalities that charm you almost instantly, and Omar was one such man. He was the kind of conversationalist who didn't try to impress the other person, who just eased them into a chat that felt oddly comforting. When he was dropping Ananda near the Alexandria Library, Ananda couldn't help but thank him and, in the same breath, ask if he was free to meet for a drink that evening. Omar noted down his number on his cell phone and said he'd text him an address.

Roaming its multiple levels, Ananda spent the entire day revelling in the library's quiet grandeur. He couldn't recall how long he had stood in front of a bust of the illustrious Egyptian writer Naguib Mahfouz, one of the earliest practitioners of contemporary Arabic literature, staring into its eyes, hoping it would come to life for a brief moment.

After an intense and deeply satisfying day at the library, at around 8 p.m., he found himself in the company of Omar inside a place that closely resembled just about any regular British pub. Ananda was, by his own admission, 'the academic type'. While Omar was a sales manager at an American industrial tools manufacturing company. There was no apparent reason why they should have got along so quickly, but the truth was they did.

One didn't have a clue about industrial tools, the other stayed far away from academia. And they discovered after the second drink, post an exchange of general pleasantries, that finding common ground was not going to be easy. So they chose to talk about what brought them together in the first place: Bollywood. And their mutual love for Dev Anand and Guru Dutt. Omar's distaste for overtly sentimental Rajesh Khanna blockbusters, their mutual belief that Smita Patil and Naseeruddin Shah were the best actors that Hindi cinema has ever produced. Some Champions League game was being telecast live on the telly, and one of Egypt's darling sons was playing. So naturally, nearly the entire place was in a celebratory mood. Laughing, singing, cheering for their hero.

Even though their worlds were far apart, both Ananda and Omar were aware that they were stuck inside tiny boxes of the respective roles they played in the world outside that pub. One as a famed academic, the other as a loaded salesman. But around each other they had suddenly discovered this opportunity to go completely against their predictable nature and momentarily become what they could not be in their own circles. They were certain their paths would possibly never collide again, and once they parted with a firm handshake and maybe a hug, they would never see each other again in the future. It felt to them like a one-night stand that didn't involve any sex. Instead, one that presented two men with a chance to let go. By the end of the night, when they insisted the DJ play a song from the famous Hindi film *Masoom* and danced to it holding each other's hand, neither were surprised by their own behaviour.

They stayed long after the match on the television had finished and everyone else had left, drinking deep into the night. Finally, when the bar owners had to politely throw them out, because they had to shut down the place, the song *Huzoor is kadar bhi na itraake chaliye* was still firmly stuck in their heads and on their lips. A most unlikely short-term association, that to an outsider would have looked like a friendship, had blossomed out of nowhere.

When Omar dropped Ananda back at his hotel that night, he insisted that Ananda come over to his home for lunch the next day. Ananda had a train to catch at around ten in the night and had kept the day free to roam around the city, check out the historic Citadel of Qaitbay or visit the abandoned ruins of the Lighthouse of Alexandria – one of the seven wonders of the ancient world destroyed by colossal earthquakes in the 1300s. But he couldn't say no to Omar. In return, Omar promised him a hearty meal of koshary, the country's national dish and vastly popular street food.

Most people would have embraced their bed and retired for the night after such a long day, but that cliche about writers and insomnia is popular because it's true. After a quick shower, Ananda sat down on the couch next to the hotel bed and took out his phone. There were a few messages, a couple of missed calls, notifications to update some apps on his phone. Habitually, he ignored them without blinking an eye. He was about to put the device away when he noticed there was a friend request on Facebook from Omar Siddiqui. His eyes were tired, but curiosity got the better of him and he opened Omar's profile, going straight to his photo albums to see what his life looked like at a glance.

To his disappointment, it was more of the same things that he so vehemently detested about social media. Pictures of him taking trips to some mountain town, of celebrating maybe a promotion with friends in a bar, some pictures underwater with him making the thumbs-up sign to the camera as if without his approval all marine life would cease to exist. Vacations, night outs, festivals. The dizzying velocity and zest with which nearly every life moved on social networks, unfolding in high points only and never a dip, manifested in front of Ananda with each push of a button. Ananda yawned. At least it was boring enough to make him sleepy, and he was thankful to Omar for that. He was about to close the page when his eyes went towards a face in the background in one of Omar's family photographs.

When he scrolled through the page once again, he noticed the same face appear in a few more photographs. Never the focal point of the pictures, only sometimes resurfacing in a corner, or behind a group of people posing, and once in a mirror as a reflection. Nebulous, almost otherworldly. Like a ghost who just happened to be there when the photographs were being taken. The camera capturing her without seeking her permission.

Ananda didn't need to see her face any more clearly though; even in the mist of those bleary images, he knew who he was looking at. Hundreds of likes and comments were visible on each of the pictures, and yet none could have been for her. There were very few people in the world who could have spotted Devaki in those pictures.

At first, he felt a sense of shock, the sudden unexpectedness with which she had returned to his life. Much like how she had left. And soon after, he breathed a sigh of relief. To learn that she was alive, in an entirely new habitat, but she wouldn't stay in a place where she couldn't make at least a few genuine connections for too long. Ananda was hopeful she had managed to do that there.

Instinctively, he opened his phone book and dialled Omar's number. He needed to tell Omar about Devaki's truth, of course. Then ask for his help to find her, if she was still in Egypt. If she was in so many of his pictures, they must share some kind of a relationship. Although from the photographs, it was hard to tell the nature of it. Friends, lovers, flatmates – it didn't matter to Ananda. All he wanted to do was see her one more time. After all this time. Tell her how much he had missed having her around – her vigour, her sense of wonder, her audacity to live life on her own terms.

She would surely be happy to see him too.

But when Omar picked up and said, 'Hello,' something turned inside Ananda. A glitch in his mind from the deep recesses of memory shrouded his heart. If she would have wanted to see him, wouldn't she have tried at least once in all these years to seek him out? Devaki had gone away, but Ananda was still exactly where she had left him. The same house address, the same telephone number, the same streets, the same favourite restaurants, the same routines. She knew everything that his life was made of.

And yet.

Besides, what if he was wrong? Yes, he could identify Devaki in the middle of a thousand similar faces, but none of the photographs in front of him showed the woman's face with absolute clarity. Even if there was a slim chance that he was wrong, it would be highly embarrassing for him to face Omar after making such an absurd claim. And what if it was her, and she did not want to be seen by those who knew her before she built a new life here? Far away from the place where she was born, where perhaps she could never find her home.

That is why when Omar said, 'Hello,' in a sombre, restful voice, Ananda informed him that he wouldn't be able to make it to his home the next day. He had something urgent to attend to back home and had to take the earliest possible flight to India. Omar didn't enquire what the urgent thing was, told him how lovely it was to have met him, then asked him to stay in touch and disconnected.

On his way to the airport the following evening, Ananda opened one of the images on his phone that he had saved from Omar's profile. Many happy faces were sitting at a table next to a lake and enjoying a meal, and somewhere behind them a solitary woman was walking towards the water. He wished that her days of raging against the dying of the light were finally behind her. And what lay ahead was a vast sea where she finally felt light … where she could float with nothing but the sky, the water and the earth enveloping her.

Ananda whispered goodbye to Devaki under his breath and deleted the photo from his phone.

Acknowledgements

Prantik, for dreaming impossible dreams with me for more than two decades and knowing how to repair audio cassettes. Athena, for picking me up at the New Delhi railway station that day when I had nowhere to go. Aldeena, for being my first teacher and first friend in publishing. Himanjali, for reminding me that it is possible to do important things without carrying the needless cross of seriousness. Megha and Abhay, for being the two reasons I behave like a somewhat sane person in the office. Satadru and Rahul, for becoming warm blankets on the chilliest days. Amrita, Tanima, Shreya for letting me be the fourth wheel once a year. Priyata, for bearing with me for as long as it is humanly possible, the endless laughs amidst the madness and your infectious kindness.

Chirag Thakkar, my editor, for believing in this novel on days when even I couldn't. Chakrika, my copy editor, for showing so much care to every sentence in this novel and making my work readable. Malvika Tewari, for the haunting cover. Meenakshi Singh and her team, for all their marketing and publicity wizardry to spread the word about this little book. Kanishka Gupta, my literary agent, for patiently championing this novel since its inception and not giving up on it. Rahul Srivastava, managing director at Bloomsbury India, for quietly ensuring this novel gets the best home it could ask for.

My grandfather, for letting me borrow books from his home library at an age when I shouldn't have been reading the books that were in his home library. Souvik and Anurag, for being my first and, so far, only babies. My parents, for always believing that I'll turn out all right even though there was overwhelming evidence that suggested otherwise; especially my mother, for introducing me to most things I know and love.

Every stranger who left me alone, whether on a park bench or on a train journey or at a cinema, and helped me protect my solitude. Every single bookstore in the world, and/or elsewhere.

Bob Dylan.

Teju Cole, Wendy Cope, Jim Jarmusch.

Saul Leiter, Joan Baez, Safdar Hashmi.

And Pushkin.